Hark! The Herald Angel Falls

Good intentions
die unless they
are executed.

—Amish Proverb

Hark! The Herald Angel Falls

TRICIA GOYER

Sugarcreek Amish Mysteries is a trademark of Guideposts.

Published by Guideposts Books & Inspirational Media
100 Reserve Road, Suite E200
Danbury, CT 06810
Guideposts.org

This is a work of fiction. Sugarcreek, Ohio, actually exists and some characters are based on actual residents whose identities have been fictionalized to protect their privacy. All other names, characters, businesses, and events are the creation of the author's imagination, and any resemblance to actual persons or events is coincidental.

Every attempt has been made to credit the sources of copyrighted material used in this book. If any such acknowledgment has been inadvertently omitted or miscredited, receipt of such information would be appreciated.

Scripture references are from the following sources: The Holy Bible, King James Version (KJV). *The Holy Bible, New International Version*®, NIV®. Copyright © 1973, 1978, 1984 by International Bible Society. Used by permission of Zondervan.

Cover and interior design by Müllerhaus
Cover illustration by Bob Kayganich, represented by Illustration Online LLC.
Typeset by Aptara, Inc.

Printed and bound in the United States of America
10 9 8 7 6 5 4 3 2 1

CHAPTER ONE

Cheryl Miller opened the front door and stepped out, noting that the front porch steps needed to be shoveled off yet again. Icy air hit her cheeks, and a shiver ran down her spine. At least another half-inch of snow had fallen in the five hours since Levi had left bright and early. Yet only a few flakes fell now—not enough to stop the community from gathering around the new, life-size nativity scene Levi had built at Community Bible Church, on the corner of Church Street and Main Street near downtown Sugarcreek.

The community had come together to create a live nativity that would last until Christmas Eve, and today's noon celebration officially kicked off the event. Sugarcreek always seemed to come alive during the festivities. With the Swiss architectural styles and the giant cuckoo clock downtown decorated for Christmas, tourists swarmed to the quaint area during the holidays. Adding a drive-by nativity with live characters was yet another way to welcome shoppers and out-of-towners to the heart of their town.

Today, the community would gather to see church members dressed up as the familiar biblical characters and to enjoy hot cocoa and cookies. Even though the day proved nippy, the festival celebration was worth it as the people of Sugarcreek and beyond would be reminded of the true meaning of Christmas.

And I need to be reminded of the true meaning of Christmas, Cheryl told herself, stepping back inside and shutting the door. Her life was full of so many wonderful things, yet in the busyness of the day-to-day, it was easy to forget to slow down, enjoy the people around her, and remember to turn her heart toward God and His goodness, no matter what filled her day.

Cheryl was looking forward to things slowing down now that Levi's big project was finished. After today, she'd have him around the farm more to help with the kids, which meant she could tackle the Christmas shopping and baking she'd been putting off.

As head of the live nativity building project, Levi had done his best to build a sturdy structure and make it comfortable for those who would participate in the manger scene every evening until Christmas. Just this morning, as he finished his last sip of coffee, he told Cheryl he'd tucked a gas-powered heater safely behind the manger so Mary, Joseph, and any visiting sheep could stay warm. Of course her thoughtful husband would think of that.

Cheryl glanced at her watch. She and the kids had better get moving if they were going to make it by noon. She had forty-five minutes before the nativity program started. She would shovel the steps, get her kids dressed, and somehow make it to town. She sighed. She seemed to be running behind on everything these days.

Soon things will be back to normal.

Cheryl grabbed Levi's jacket by the front door and slipped it on then slid her feet into her snow boots. The jingle of coins and other odd pieces in Levi's pockets caused her to smile. That was one of the things she'd learned about Levi in the years they'd been married. He found every odd bit useful and never threw anything away. "I never know when I'll need something like this," he'd repeat time and again.

As Cheryl prepared to go outside, Rebecca raced up to her. Cheryl smiled at the six-year-old's disheveled hair with curls looping in every direction. Cheryl didn't want to think about her own hair. She knew it was equally a mess. She hadn't run a brush through it since waking up hours ago.

"Thank goodness for hat weather," she mumbled under her breath. Yes, her bright red beanie would come in handy today. Cheryl quickly put it on, tucking her hair inside.

Rebecca tilted her head, curiously eyeing her. "Where are you going?"

Cheryl opened the door, and a swirl of snow rushed in with a blast of wind. "To shovel the steps. It'll take just a minute. And then we're getting in the car for our special outing, remember?"

Rebecca's eyes brightened at the winter wonderland outside the door. "Oh, pretty!"

Cheryl looked down and noticed that Rebecca had only one sock on, and her boots were nowhere in sight. "Your pretty little toes will freeze if you don't finish getting dressed. Didn't I tell you to get some pants and socks on? Oh, and find your coat and boots too. As soon as I clear off this porch we'll be heading out."

"Mommy, look!" Rebecca's squeal pierced the air. Cheryl followed her daughter's gaze to a package on the porch. Airmail labels added a punch of color to the brown box.

"It looks like something from Aunt Mitzi." Cheryl bent down, picked it up, and quickly set it just inside the door. "I'll be right back. Find your boots and coat, okay?"

It took Cheryl no time at all to shovel a pathway down the steps. She would let Levi finish the rest when they returned together that afternoon. He'd get their whole porch and walkway done quickly, and he'd most likely have a smile on his face as he went about his work.

Back inside, Cheryl saw that Rebecca had placed the box on the dining room table.

Rebecca pointed, and her nose crinkled as she smiled. "Aunt Mitzi sent us Christmas presents!"

"You're right. All the way from the other side of the world." Cheryl turned the box to appreciate the variety of postal labels. "Our first Christmas presents this year, delivered right to our doorstep."

Rebecca pointed to the foreign words written in red, in Aunt Mitzi's perfect handwriting, on the side of the box. "What does that say?"

"Well, I actually know this phrase. The last word gives it away. It says '*Bikpela hamamas blong dispela Krismas*,'" Cheryl read, although she was sure she'd mispronounced every word. She smiled, thinking about how her aunt spoke Tok Pisin more often than English in her work in Papua New Guinea. "That means 'Merry Christmas.'"

Rebecca clapped her hands. "Can we open the box?"

"Later, I promise. We're going to go see the live nativity, remember? The angel, Mary, Joseph, and the shepherds will be there. And maybe even sheep. There will be treats for us too." At the mention of the treats, Cheryl paused and looked around. Where was Matthew? Her son was being awfully quiet. If he had been anywhere in earshot, he would have immediately started asking for a treat to take in his pocket for the ride. He asked for one for every car ride, and the napkins on her car's back seat floorboard proved it.

"Matthew's brushing his teeth!" Rebecca exclaimed. Cheryl winced and hurried to the bathroom. She should have been paying closer attention. When had she thought having two kids would be a breeze? Not since the first day they brought Matthew home, that was for sure.

If only I had my act together like Aunt Mitzi, Cheryl scolded herself as she rushed into the bathroom. Three-year-old Matthew smiled at her. His teeth were indeed shiny. Then again, toothpaste covered everything in sight—Matthew's face, the sink, even the tile floor beneath her feet.

Cheryl forced a smile. "Oh Matthew, sweet boy. You're supposed to let Mommy help you, aren't you?"

For the briefest moment, she considered texting Levi and telling him they wouldn't make it to the nativity program today after all, but she knew he would be disappointed. He'd given so much time over the last week to build the set and work with others from the local churches to ensure that everything was perfect. It had been wonderful to see him spending time with new friends, especially when she knew a part of him still felt a little homesick after leaving the Amish.

It took Cheryl a few minutes to get Matthew cleaned up. The bathroom would have to wait. She quickly got him into his jacket and boots. When he was ready, Cheryl was pleasantly surprised to see Rebecca dressed in her boots and coat and standing by the table, eyeing the box from Aunt Mitzi. Beau sat on the table next to the box and fixed his crystal-blue eyes on Cheryl as if he too expected a gift.

Rebecca pointed to the box. "Look, Matthew, Auntie Mitzi sent us presents. Maybe there's one for you or maybe even twooo." She grinned as she drew out the last syllable.

Matthew's eyes widened. "Pwesent for me? Peas?"

Cheryl smiled at her son's toddler speech. "That was nice of you to say *please*." She was about to tell them again that they'd open the box when they got home, but the joy on her children's faces made her give in.

"All right, I'll open the box, but then we have to be on our way. This will only take a minute, right?" she said more to herself than them.

Cheryl found a pair of scissors and cut the tape. A half-dozen small, wrapped packages were nestled inside the box.

She pulled one out, noting the name. "Rebecca, this present is for you." Even though it was only wrapped in simple brown paper, Rebecca beamed. Cheryl pulled another of equal size out of the box. "And Matthew, here's one for you."

Cheryl pulled a larger package from the box, expecting her name or Levi's. Instead, she saw an unexpected name. *Sarah Miller-Bradley*. Cheryl hadn't seen that name in a while. Not that they hadn't tried to reach out to Levi's sister. As the years had passed, Sarah leaving the Amish to marry an *Englischer* became less of an issue. And then, when Levi had done the same, Cheryl had seen a significant shift in Seth and Naomi, Levi and Sarah's parents. As much as her in-laws still stood by their Amish ways, they maintained a close relationship with her and Levi and the children. Naomi often spoke about how she wanted a closer relationship with Sarah.

How interesting that Aunt Mitzi included a present for Sarah in their box this year.

The clock on the kitchen wall ticked away the time, and Cheryl hurriedly pulled out the next present. This one had the name *Joe* on it, Sarah's husband. The next two gifts had the names she expected on them, *Levi* and *Cheryl*. The final small package had the name *Beau*.

As she lined the presents up on the table, something stirred within Cheryl's heart. She did not doubt that Aunt Mitzi prayed for her, her husband, and her children daily. She also believed that Aunt Mitzi prayed for their extended family too. These gifts demonstrated her love and concern. And now Cheryl had an excellent excuse to reach out to Levi's sister. She smiled at the thought.

"My pwesent!" Matthew said, pointing to his gift.

Beau meowed, as if scolding Matthew for being too loud, and then jumped off the table and sauntered off.

"Yes, and as soon as we get a tree, we'll put these presents under it." Cheryl plopped a knitted cap on her son's head. Then, motioning for Rebecca to follow her to the door, Cheryl scooped Matthew up and put him on her hip. "We'll work on the tree and the presents later, but right now we have to get to town and see the big, big stable your daddy made."

"I want pwesent!" Matthew lunged for the package. Cheryl ignored his efforts, righted him, and hurried to the door.

"We're going to see Daddy and all the sheep and the big nativity set, remember? Daddy's been working so hard on it. We have to hurry. We don't want to be late." Thankfully, the mention of sheep grabbed Matthew's attention.

"Sheep, sheep!" he called as she buckled him into his car seat. When Matthew was secure, Cheryl helped Rebecca buckle hers.

Cheryl tried not to play the comparison game as she drove to town, but it was hard. Aunt Mitzi always seemed to be on top of things. She must have started putting together their Christmas box months ago. Cheryl had yet to purchase one gift for Levi and the children, let alone her extended family. Of course, Naomi would say that things were always a little bit more challenging with little ones underfoot.

"These are the best years of your life." Her mother-in-law's familiar words replayed in Cheryl's mind. And they were true. After so many years of wondering if she'd ever get the family she dreamed of, Cheryl had to remind herself that she had all she'd prayed for, and they were named Rebecca, Matthew, and Levi.

Cheryl hummed a Christmas carol as she drove, choosing to keep a happy attitude and a thankful heart, despite the strain of the past week. Before she'd married Levi, she'd been drawn to his caring nature, giving attitude, and strong work ethic. She wouldn't fault him for that now.

Fifteen minutes later, Cheryl had parked the car and gotten the kids out of their car seats. She smiled to herself, amazed that she'd gotten to the event on time. It was only when she adjusted her scarf that she realized she was wearing Levi's coat instead of her own. She had put it on to shovel the walk and must have grabbed it and thrown it on without thinking when she'd rushed out the door with the kids. She must look a fright. Oh well. She'd fit right in with the shepherds and their sheep.

The ring of a hammer echoed in the air as Cheryl approached the front lawn of Community Bible Church.

"Daddy! I see him!" Rebecca bounced at Cheryl's side, squeezing her gloved hand tighter.

Cheryl paused, looking up at the barnlike structure. Sure enough, Levi was hammering up a piece of the stable that must have fallen off. Cheryl released a low whistle. It looked like there were over a hundred people in the crowd standing on the lawn between the parking lot and the nativity set.

Just as Levi finished and slipped his hammer into his tool belt loop, the bleating of an escaped sheep caught his attention. He immediately took off after it. A fully dressed wise man joined the chase. Laughter from the crowd moved in a wave across the lawn as more people caught sight of the mishap.

Rebecca tugged on Cheryl's hand, pulling in the direction of the crowd. "Can we go see Daddy?"

"Not yet, Boo. It looks like he's busy helping one of the wise men round up that stray sheep."

Rebecca bounced on her toes, her boots making a squeaky sound on the snow. "Is that barn going to stay at the church always?"

"It does look like a barn, doesn't it? It's a nativity set, just like the little one we have at home."

Rebecca's eyes widened. "That's going to have to be a big baby Jesus."

Cheryl laughed. "It's going to be a pretty big baby doll. But it'll be more like one of the dollies you play with, not a ceramic one like in our nativity set."

Rebecca didn't respond to Cheryl's comment about the doll, and Cheryl knew her daughter's mind had already moved on to other things, likely the huge red ornaments that hung in the pine tree just to the left of the nativity set and the long table laden with steaming hot cocoa and cookies next to the tree. Sure enough, Rebecca began to pull in that direction, and Cheryl followed with Matthew in tow.

Cheryl's eyes widened when she noticed a familiar person standing near the cookie display. She gasped. "It can't be," she said to herself. After all these years. *How in the world did Aunt Mitzi know?*

Chapter Two

"Cookies, cookies, peas!" Matthew cried out. He lunged toward the table with every ounce of energy, and Cheryl did her best to keep him from cutting in line.

"Yes, Matthew. Just a minute." A funny feeling stirred in Cheryl's stomach as she looked at the dark-haired woman who stood at the table, seeming to study the cookie options. Sarah wore baggy jeans and a puffy black jacket. Her long hair fell down her back, and a gray slouch hat added a nice touch, making her appear like a model from a clothing ad.

How could this be? Just an hour ago, Cheryl had opened that box from Aunt Mitzi and found gifts for Sarah and Joe. Had she known they would be coming around this Christmas? Of course not. She couldn't have known that. Yet there was Sarah, standing right in front of her.

Cheryl smiled. Aunt Mitzi had a close relationship with God. Maybe He had whispered the surprise to her. It seemed like just the type of thing He would do.

Cheryl tightened her grip on her children's hands and hurried toward the cookie table. Just before she reached it, she stopped, leaned down so that her mouth was close to Rebecca's ear, and pointed with her chin. "Rebecca, look."

Rebecca peeked around Cheryl's jacket. Her eyebrows furrowed as she spotted Sarah, who was now enjoying a sugar cookie with pink frosting. "That lady looks like Aunt Elizabeth. But I know it's not."

At that moment Sarah spotted Cheryl and the kids.

Sarah's eyes widened. "Cheryl! Rebecca! And that can't be Matthew, can it?" She rushed up to them, shaking her head in disbelief. "Cheryl, is that really you?" Sarah looked a bit older than the last time Cheryl had seen her. How many years had it been? Far too many.

Cheryl smiled and rushed forward. "Yes, it's us. How could we miss out on one of the most exciting things happening in Sugarcreek? What brings you here?" She released the children's hands and pulled Sarah into an embrace. "It's so good to see you."

"I was hoping I would see you here. Yes, exciting times in Sugarcreek. Is Levi around?"

"Last time I spotted Levi, he was chasing a sheep. I'm sure we'll be able to catch up with him soon. He came early this morning to finish things up. He built the whole set." Cheryl waved toward the stable-like building that was just starting to fill up with the cast for the nativity scene. "I know Levi will be excited to see you too."

As Cheryl talked, Sarah's husband, Joe, approached. He was tall with dark hair and intense brown eyes. Sarah stiffened slightly as he neared, and at the same moment Cheryl noticed the scowl on Joe's face, Sarah shrank back even more.

"Oh, that sounds just like Levi." Sarah's smile seemed forced. "We'll make sure to look for him."

"So how long are you going to be in town?" Cheryl dared to ask. "We would love to have you over."

"Actually, we're currently renting a place over in Berlin, so not too far away." Sarah twirled a strand of hair around her finger. "We just moved down a couple of months ago. We're looking to buy property in the area. In fact, there is a farm for sale—"

Joe stepped forward, cutting Sarah off. He cleared his throat. "Listen, Sarah, we're still looking. We haven't made any decisions." His voice was stern.

"But we are looking for some type of farm. Maybe people can look around for us—"

"No." Joe almost shouted the word. "We don't need to bother people. We'll figure it out." He cleared his throat as if trying to get her attention.

"It's really no bother," Cheryl said, but it was evident that nothing she had to say would change Joe's mind. She attempted to hide her surprise at Joe's response. She hadn't spent much time with him, but when she had, he'd always been friendly. But not today. It seemed like he didn't want Sarah talking to her at all. It made her wonder why the couple was moving closer. What would be the point if they didn't want to spend time with family?

Cheryl's mind raced, trying to figure out what to say, what to do. She also considered mentioning that, just today, Christmas presents had arrived from Aunt Mitzi for the two of them. But again, the look on Joe's face gave her pause.

"Yes, well, if you're around and you have time, just let us know," Cheryl repeated. "We would love to have you both."

Sarah nodded and smiled, but from the pinched look on her face, Cheryl could tell she had other things on her mind.

Joe wrapped his hand around Sarah's gloved one. "Listen, we need to go, Sarah. The person we're supposed to meet just drove up."

Cheryl offered a parting wave, and Sarah returned it. It was only after they hurried away that Rebecca piped up. "Who was that?"

"Oh dear." Cheryl looked down at her daughter. "You haven't seen your aunt Sarah in a while, have you?"

Rebecca's nose wrinkled up, and her brow furrowed. "I know Auntie Elizabeth and Auntie Esther, but I don't remember Auntie Sarah."

"Auntie Sarah is younger than your daddy but older than Auntie Elizabeth and Auntie Esther. She moved away a long time ago, before you were born. She's only been at family gatherings a few times. That's probably why you don't remember her."

Cheryl watched as Joe clung to Sarah's hand and pulled her along, weaving through the crowd. Then, finally, they hurried out to the parking lot.

They walked toward a red pickup, and, as Cheryl watched, a young man jumped out of the truck and ran his hand through his sandy-colored hair. Cheryl looked closer and realized she knew him. It was Owen, the son of their neighbor, Rudy Wight. Sarah had mentioned that she and Joe were looking for property in the area. Were they interested in Rudy's property right next to her and Levi's place?

The idea both thrilled and worried Cheryl. It was so good to see Sarah, but something had happened with Joe. He had looked at Cheryl as if he didn't know her. He had also seemed bothered that

Sarah was talking to her. Did Joe have a problem with the family now? Maybe it was because Levi had also left the Amish, but he hadn't received the same poor treatment that Sarah had from their father, especially in the early years when she had first left.

Yet the situations were different. When Sarah had chosen to leave their family's Amish ways, she had gone out of rebellion, choosing to follow her own path and rejecting the ways of her family. On the other hand, Levi had talked to his parents concerning his growing feelings for Cheryl for many months before he decided to pursue her. He had taken things slowly. He had sought his parents' advice. Didn't Joe understand that?

Cheryl thought about the property next to them. There was a beautiful house and at least ten acres. She believed it had been for sale recently. But maybe she was mistaken. It was hard to keep track of everything happening in the outside world when so much was happening inside her own home, with these two very busy kids.

She also remembered that Levi had gone over to talk to Rudy Wight recently. So indeed, if Levi had known that Sarah and Joe wanted to move closer, he would have said something to her. She made a mental note to ask Levi about it later that night. But, for now, she would enjoy this time with her kids, the cookies with the hot cocoa, and seeing the joy that Levi's work on the nativity set brought to so many people.

Cheryl felt a tug on her jacket. She looked down to see that Rebecca still stood next to her. Suddenly, she realized that she was no longer holding Matthew's hand. She gasped and turned quickly, scanning the crowd for her son. Panic rose in her throat. She looked toward the nativity set, where the cast members were congregating. Matthew was nowhere in sight.

"Matthew's eating all the cookies!" Rebecca shouted, and Cheryl released the breath she'd been holding. She turned back to the table with the cocoa and cookies. Sure enough, Matthew stood there with four cookies in his hand. Another cookie filled his mouth, stuffed in his cheeks.

Cheryl was just about to scold Matthew when she felt Rebecca's tug again. "Mommy, look, everyone's going to the stable. And look! They have all the sheep!"

Cheryl took the extra cookies from Matthew, wrapped them in a napkin, and tucked them in her coat pocket on top of the random bits of twine and bolts. She scooted her way toward the front so the children could get a good view. In the center of the stable was a manger filled with hay, and a large baby doll was snuggled inside the cradle. Behind the manger, a man and a woman stood in full costume. Gentle smiles were on their faces as they looked down at the swaddled baby. To the right of the woman stood two shepherds, one tall and one short. And sure enough, next to them, three sheep huddled up. They lingered close to the manger, and Cheryl guessed it was because of the warmth from the heater.

Still holding Matthew's and Rebecca's hands, Cheryl moved closer to the nativity set. Now, where was Levi?

Her smile fell when she spotted him, facing off with an angel, his shoulders squared.

"Do you see Daddy?" Rebecca asked.

Almost as if on cue, Levi's voice rose over the chattering crowd. "Now, Rudy, we don't need to go into that here." He didn't sound happy. Rebecca tugged on Cheryl's hand, and Cheryl looked down at her.

"It sounds like Daddy's mad."

"Yes. It doesn't sound good." Cheryl tried to keep her tone light. Finally, she forced a smile and offered a suggestion. "Why don't we walk over there and see what's happening? And look, it seems like the nativity show is about to start."

"Now you know the trouble you've caused. I don't care where we are. We need to deal with this. You have no idea what you've done." Rudy Wight's voice split the air.

Levi raised his hands as if in surrender. "Why don't I stop by your place later?"

Rudy's halo swung as he shook his head. "No! No, no, no!"

The chattering of voices around them quieted, and all eyes turned to the two men. Rudy wore a long white gown, and he looked completely out of place next to Levi in his work clothes.

As if sensing all eyes on him, Levi forced a smile. Still, Cheryl could see the anger in his eyes. "Listen, we'll talk about this later."

Cheryl stepped closer. "Levi, is everything all right?"

Levi turned to her. His furrowed brows softened as he spotted her.

He waved. "Why don't you and the kids move up to the front so you can get a good, close look? Rebecca did you see the sheep? I will be right there. I promise."

Cheryl nodded and moved closer to the nativity scene. She could tell from the look on Levi's face he didn't want a confrontation with Rudy, especially in front of the kids, but the intensity in his eyes told her that things were not all right.

The choir director from Cheryl's church rushed forward and stepped between Levi and Rudy. He leaned close to Rudy and spoke in a low voice. Cheryl couldn't hear what was being said, but she could see the resignation on Rudy's face before he turned and walked toward the stable.

Off to the side, a small choir began to sing "Silent Night," and Cheryl saw movement near the back of the stable. She couldn't see a ladder, but it was clear that Rudy was climbing up one in his long angel gown. She released the breath she was holding and tried to focus on the moment and all that it signified—hope, peace, and the joy of the Christmas season, whether she was ready for it or not.

The tense look on Rudy's face from moments before was gone. Instead, he wore a massive smile as he climbed. Finally, he reached the top of the platform and stepped onto it.

He swept his hands upwards. "Hark," he called. Just then, a horrendous crack filled the air. Rudy frowned, and then, almost in slow motion, he twisted sideways and fell from the set.

Cheryl heard a loud thump above the gasps of the crowd. The choir stopped in the middle of the stanza. Surprised screams and murmurs erupted around her. Yet from the ground beside the stable, it was frighteningly quiet.

CHAPTER THREE

"M ommy, Mommy!" Rebecca cried, gripping Cheryl's leg and hiding her face in Cheryl's jacket.

Cries of disbelief and horror rose from the crowd. The woman beside Cheryl gasped. "Did you see that? The angel, he fell."

"Is that part of the show?" someone else asked.

"Somebody call 911!" a man yelled.

The disbelieving shout of a man next to Cheryl caught her attention. She turned to see Rudy's son, Owen. His eyes were wide, and his mouth was open in fright. Cheryl expected him to run to check on his dad, but instead he turned and ran in the opposite direction, toward the road.

Cheryl checked on her children. She could tell that Matthew didn't understand, although he curiously eyed the panicked people around him. Cheryl knelt to her children's level, pressing her knee into the snow. The sound of sirens split the air.

"Is there a doctor here? Anyone?" a man shouted close to them, causing Matthew to jump. Then Matthew's pout turned into a small whimper. As more sirens joined the first, he wrapped his arms around Cheryl's neck and began to cry.

"Mommy, Mommy," Rebecca cried out again, also clinging to Cheryl. "The angel just fell. Mommy, did the angel think he could fly?"

"Back here!" Cheryl heard Levi calling. She wished she could go to him, but she knew she couldn't take the children over there. They'd seen enough already.

Cheryl pulled both of her children closer and then dared to look in the direction of her husband's shout. She was barely able to make out Levi kneeling on the snowy ground next to the crumpled body of Rudy Wight. The man's white angel gown was splayed out, blending into the snow.

Another siren filled the air, and Cheryl looked over to see Owen flagging down a police car. The officer parked, and they hurried toward the nativity set together.

Cheryl's stomach twisted into a knot, and she wished this was just a bad dream. More people from the crowd huddled together, talking and pointing. Cheryl heard sobs, and she looked to see the woman who played Mary curled against Joseph's chest. Mary was crying, and Joseph was praying.

She wanted to rush to Levi's side, but that wasn't possible. She had two children to think about. She'd heard enough stories to know that an event like this could traumatize a child for years to come.

Cheryl turned her children's faces in her direction. She attempted to keep her voice calm. "It looks like there's been an accident. I am sure Mr. Rudy will be all right. Kind emergency workers are coming to take care of him. Let's pray too, okay?"

Cheryl said a simple prayer and then stood, preparing to lead her children to the car. When she looked back, she noticed Owen and the police officer near the rear of the large stable. Instead of checking on his father, Owen pointed to Levi, his face red with anger. He said something to the officer that Cheryl couldn't make out. A sinking feeling grew in the pit of her stomach, and a chill ran down her spine. She gripped her children's hands even tighter.

"Mommy?" Rebecca watched as the officer approached Levi.

"It'll be okay. The officer just wants to talk to Daddy, that's all," Cheryl said, as much for herself as for her daughter.

More shouting from Owen, but she refused to look back again. It was hard enough seeing Rudy splayed on the ground. Why in the world would Owen direct the officer to Levi?

By the time they reached Cheryl's car, tears were flowing down Rebecca's cheeks. Cheryl opened the door and helped the kids inside. "You both are being so brave. I know it was scary seeing that. Let's sit inside until we can talk to Daddy, okay?" She reached into her pocket and pulled out the cookies that Matthew had taken from the table. "I even have cookies we can snack on."

Matthew eagerly accepted another cookie and climbed into his car seat, but Rebecca looked at the cookie dejectedly and shook her head. "But Daddy…" Her voice came out in a squeaky cry.

"It'll be okay," Cheryl repeated. "He's just going to stay there to make sure the men take care of Mr. Rudy. I'm going to start the car to keep us warm."

An ambulance pulled up right as Cheryl got into the front seat, started the car, and turned on the heat. From the rearview mirror, she saw Rebecca watching with wide eyes as the paramedics rushed a stretcher toward the nativity scene.

Almost immediately, Cheryl regretted giving Matthew yet another cookie full of sugar and allowing him to remain unbuckled. Within a minute, her stocky toddler was climbing from the back seat up to the front passenger seat and then back again. For a few minutes, Rebecca kept a lookout for her daddy and then finally decided to join her brother. Soon cookie crumbs were scattered throughout the vehicle's interior, but all Cheryl could think about was Rudy. How seriously was he hurt? She knew it had to be critical. After his fall, there had been no shouts of fear or cries of pain. The silence had been the worst part.

Cheryl also worried about Levi. He had a tender soul, and she knew that even though he and Rudy had been having some type of disagreement just moments before, Levi would be very concerned about their neighbor.

As they waited, the crowd thinned out. Instead of the celebration everyone had anticipated, there were only worried looks and frowns on people's faces.

Finally, there was movement from the side of the stable. Cheryl watched as the paramedics wheeled the stretcher to the ambulance and then lifted it inside. Then, with sirens blaring, they drove away.

It wasn't until the ambulance had left that Cheryl realized another police car had arrived at the scene. Four officers were now in the area. One officer was talking with Levi. A second was carefully reviewing the scene. The other two officers had fanned out, interviewing clusters of witnesses.

Cheryl just hoped that someone else had witnessed the incident more clearly. Even though she hadn't been but about fifteen feet away, she hadn't seen what had caused Rudy to fall. She'd only seen his body shift with the uplifting of his arms, and she'd heard a loud crack. And then he fell.

Had Rudy lost his balance? Had his feet tripped over his long angel robes? Yet, if that was the case, what had caused that cracking sound?

More people walked to the parking lot. Two women stood beside the car parked next to Cheryl's. They were talking about the incident. Cheryl cracked her window to hear their words.

One of the women looked as if she'd been crying. "The officers are blocking off the area. I used to work in the police department. They're investigating the scene as a crime. They don't think this was an accident."

"Oh Georgia, you haven't worked for a police department for twenty years," the shorter woman with a white puffy hat and bright red lipstick responded. "This is Sugarcreek. I'm sure it was just an accident."

"Then you must not have heard what those officers were saying," Georgia replied with fervor. "They said there weren't enough screws holding up that platform. It wasn't anchored properly to the frame."

Not enough screws? That was impossible. Cheryl's heart hammered as she remembered the fight between Rudy and Levi just moments before the accident.

A new fear pierced her heart, and suddenly she understood better why the police were talking to Levi. *They think he did it.*

The children continued to climb back and forth over the seat, their volume rising as they did. Cheryl turned her attention to the scene across the lawn, trying not to let the noise annoy her. Owen

Wight still waved his arms as he pointed at the broken platform and then to Levi. Surely Owen didn't believe Levi had anything to do with this. Levi always did fine work. There was no way he would have constructed something so flimsy that a man would fall.

As Cheryl watched, Levi followed the officer to a patrol car. Then, out of the corner of her eye, an Amish couple walking toward the nativity set caught her attention. She recognized their sure strides and the green scarf and black coat. *Naomi! Seth!* It was so good to see Levi's parents. Cheryl knew they were also trying to figure out what was happening.

Cheryl opened the door and stood, calling to them. Her in-laws turned in her direction. Instead of the usual smiles, concern shadowed their faces. Cheryl swallowed her emotion and waved her hand, motioning them to come in her direction. She leaned in, turned off the car, and waited for them. Then she gently closed the door as they neared. Her father- and mother-in-law approached with quick steps.

"Cheryl, do you know what is happening?" Seth asked, urgency in his voice. "We were down at the Swiss Miss, picking up Esther from work, when some of our friends from the community told us there had been an accident. They said Levi was involved somehow."

"Yes, there was an accident." Cheryl scraped off a piece of ice clinging to her side window. "I—I don't understand just what happened. Levi built the nativity set, and there was an accident. Rudy Wight, our neighbor, was the angel." The words tumbled out of Cheryl's mouth. "Rudy climbed up and then just fell. I heard someone say that there weren't enough screws holding up the platform. But that's not possible. Levi built it, and I'm worried they're going to blame him."

Cheryl caught her breath, hoping Seth and Naomi had followed all that. It was quiet in the car now, and she had no doubt her children were straining to listen to figure out why the adults were so upset.

Naomi's brows furrowed. "How could they blame Levi for an accident?"

Cheryl swallowed the lump in her throat. "I'm not sure, but it has me worried all the same."

"This is worse than I imagined," Seth finally said.

Naomi looked over to where the police had assembled. "And is that Levi over there talking to them now?"

"Yes. Let's hope he's there to try to help them figure out what happened. Let's hope that my fears are for nothing, and that within a matter of minutes he'll be able to join us and come home."

The kids had given up trying to be patient and were again climbing back and forth over the seats.

Naomi leaned close to the car window and waved. Then she straightened and turned to Cheryl. "Did the children see anything? They did not see your neighbor fall, did they?"

"It all happened so fast...." Cheryl crossed her arms and hugged herself. "I'm worried because I know they're watching all of this too." She waved her hand toward Levi and the police. "I can't even imagine all the questions Rebecca's going to ask when we get home about why Daddy was talking to the police."

Seth and Naomi glanced over to where the police officer still talked to Levi, and then they looked at each other. From the looks in their eyes, Cheryl could tell a conversation had happened within the space of three heartbeats.

"We are on our way home anyway. We can go ahead and take the children with us," Naomi offered. "You know how much they love to ride in the buggy."

Cheryl released a breath, feeling a burden fall off her shoulders. "Oh, would you? Would you do that for me? You're right. They love riding in the buggy. It will help them get their minds off what happened today. And it'll give me a chance to talk to Levi. I need to figure out what's going on."

Rebecca and Matthew were happy to hear they were going to their grandparents' house. They were even more excited to hear that they would be able to ride in the buggy on the way there.

"In a couple of weeks, if it keeps snowing like this, we will be able to put the sled runners on the buggy," Seth told Matthew as he scooped up the young boy. "Then we can go dashing through the snow on a sled."

Naomi peered down at Rebecca as she took her hand. "Won't you love that, Rebecca? Sled rides are wonderful."

Rebecca nodded and allowed her grandmother to lead her away, but not before Cheryl saw fear in her daughter's eyes. Cheryl knew that Rebecca was worried about Mr. Rudy and her daddy. Cheryl understood her daughter, because she felt the same.

Chapter Four

One minute after Seth and Naomi left with the kids, Cheryl spotted Levi making his way over to her, a policeman by his side. As they approached, she noticed her husband eyeing her jacket. Looking down, she realized she still wore his work jacket, which she hadn't washed in months.

"I know I look quite the mess. I—" Cheryl was about to explain that she'd put it on to shovel the front steps, but the look on Levi's face caused her to pause. She reached out her hand to him, but instead of taking it, he frowned. And then he slowly shook his head and lowered his gaze.

Instead of Levi talking, it was the police officer who cleared his throat. "Ma'am, I'm sorry to have to say this, but I need to take your husband down to the station for questioning. Do you think you can follow?" His words hung thick and heavy in the nippy air.

"Follow? Questioning? I don't—I don't understand," she rasped. "What do you mean by taking my husband to the police station?" Cheryl looked at her husband. "Levi, are they asking you to go down there because you were close to Rudy when he fell? Did you see what happened? Did you see how he fell?"

Levi looked at her with sadness in his blue eyes. "I wish I could explain, but I cannot."

Cheryl eyed the police officer.

"Ma'am, your husband admitted he was the one who built that platform. I can't tell you more than that. But if you would follow us down there, I'd greatly appreciate it."

"Yes, Officer. Of course."

Cheryl had been to the Sugarcreek Police Department numerous times but never to wait while her husband was being questioned. She sat in the brown wooden chair in the waiting area. The officer at the desk didn't look familiar. He must be rather new. Even though Cheryl had her coat on, her knees quivered. She placed her hands on them, hoping to get them to still, but it was no use. Suddenly Cheryl's worries about getting everything done and prepared for Christmas didn't seem so important.

Upon arriving, Cheryl had asked at the desk if Chief Twitchell was around. The new officer said he'd gone out of town for a couple of days. A small television played in the corner, and a perky woman explained how to make the perfect pecan pie.

As she sat there, Cheryl realized she had not mentioned to Levi or to his parents that Sarah was in town. She hadn't had a chance to tell them how awkward things had been with Joe either. Something had to be going on for Joe to treat her so poorly. So far, nothing in this day was making sense.

Cheryl's phone rang, startling her. She retrieved it from her pocket and saw that Judith was calling. She'd met Judith last Christmas when Judith had saved Rebecca from freezing in a snowstorm. Cheryl smiled, thinking of the friendship she'd developed with her real-life Christmas "angel," who was back for a visit and staying in their *dawdy haus*. Judith was always available to help however she could. Still, she was another person who would need an explanation of a situation that Cheryl didn't understand herself.

"Hello?"

"Cheryl, I'm sorry to bother you, but I wanted to let you know about something odd that just happened. A man and woman stopped by the farm. They said they came to talk to you."

"Have you seen them before? Maybe neighbors or someone from church?" Cheryl shifted as the wooden chair grew more uncomfortable by the minute.

"You know I never forget a face, but these two were new to me." Judith's voice was low, as if she worried about being overheard. "They were walking around the yard toward the barn, and the young woman was talking excitedly. I surprised them when I came out of the dawdy haus. They said they had no idea someone was living there."

"That is strange." Cheryl tried to figure out who would go over to their farm and walk around so freely. Judith knew all their close friends and neighbors. "Did they say anything else?"

"I told them you would be back later, but they gave no commitment as to whether they would return. I also offered to take down their numbers, but again they said they would just try to connect with you another time."

A man and a woman? Cheryl knew that could be anyone, but she and Levi rarely had visitors unannounced. "Can you give me more details? Were they English or Amish?"

"Oh, they weren't Amish. They drove a fancy Jeep. The young woman had long dark hair. The man was tall and he asked me questions about living in the dawdy haus, which made me uncomfortable."

Cheryl tried to think of who would come by, and then Sarah popped into her mind. She hadn't seen Joe or Sarah after they left her to talk to Owen Wight. Yet it must have been a quick conversation, because not five minutes later, Owen had been standing next to her in the crowd. So either Joe and Sarah had finished their business with Owen quickly and had left, or they had also been in the crowd. Still, if they had stayed around, why hadn't they come to check on Levi or her and the kids? Also, Joe most likely would have rushed to the scene of the accident immediately, since he was in law enforcement. Or was he still? Cheryl hadn't gotten a chance to ask.

"Thank you, Judith. I knew you were my guardian angel, but I never realized you were my security guard too. I believe it was Levi's sister Sarah and her husband who stopped by. I saw them earlier today, and it's been years since they've been to the farm."

"But how could that be? She certainly wasn't Amish."

"Sarah grew up Amish, but that's a long story."

An officer approached. Cheryl looked up and smiled. Was it time to see Levi? Her heartbeat quickened at the thought.

"Judith, just a minute," Cheryl hurriedly said. "An officer wants to tell me something."

He leaned down to her, intense eyes locking on hers. "Ma'am, can you please keep your voice down? This is a public space."

Cheryl looked around the room, noting that she was the only one waiting, yet from the stern look on the officer's face, it didn't seem to matter. "Yes, Officer, of course."

"Cheryl, are you all right?" Judith's voice grew louder.

She pressed the phone tighter to her ear and lowered her voice. "I wish I could say I was. I can't go into all the details now, but there was an accident today at the church, and Levi is being held for questioning."

"And the children? Are they all right?"

"Yes, Rebecca and Matthew are with Levi's parents. Thank you for asking and for keeping an eye on things. Honestly, I have no idea when I'll be home."

"Don't worry about things here, Cheryl. I'll take care of everything. I've watched Levi do the chores a few times, just in case something happened and I needed to step in. Are you at the police station in Sugarcreek?"

"I am, and I have to say they need better chairs in the waiting area." Cheryl adjusted herself again, wishing there was some way to get more comfortable.

"Well, I bet you need some taking care of too. Just know that everything here will be watched after. I hope that will put your mind at ease."

Cheryl didn't understand what Judith's comment, *"I bet you need some taking care of too,"* meant until Kathy Snyder from the Honey Bee Café walked in fifteen minutes later with a large paper bag.

Kathy walked directly to Cheryl, compassion on her face. She offered the bag with a smile. "I heard you might need a bit of comfort food."

"What is this?" The wonderful aroma of bread and soup drifted from the bag.

"Judith told me you were here. She called and ordered some lunch for you. She said that Levi was helping with an investigation and you were waiting for him. So I put in an extra sandwich and cup of soup in case he's hungry too."

Cheryl stood and gave Kathy a hug before accepting the bag. "Thank you." Cheryl's stomach growled. "I didn't realize I was hungry until I smelled this."

"Yes, well, that's often what happens when our mind is full of worries. I heard about the accident at the nativity scene. I'm so thankful Levi's offering to help the officers."

"Well, it's not exactly that—"

Kathy's cell phone rang, and she interrupted Cheryl's words. "Oh, so sorry. I told them to call me if things got too busy. I need to run." She rushed out with a wave.

Cheryl sat down in the hard chair again, and the room seemed even quieter after Kathy left. She ate the apple butter ham-and-swiss sandwich and enjoyed the cup of tomato basil soup. Then, when she still hadn't heard anything about Levi, she approached the officer at the desk. "Excuse me, do you know when I can see my husband?"

The man shook his head. "I'm sorry. He's still being questioned."

Cheryl smiled. "Is there any way I can send lunch back?"

A look of disbelief crossed the man's face. His name tag read OFFICER CLAY MAESON. "No, ma'am." He shook his head. "That's strictly against policy."

Cheryl looked down at the bag in her hand and then back to the officer. "Well, would you like it then? That's not against policy, is it?"

Officer Maeson cocked an eyebrow at the bag.

"It's from Kathy at the Honey Bee." Cheryl pointed toward the door. "You saw her bring it in, didn't you?"

The man sniffed the air and breathed in deeply. "Is that tomato basil?"

"Yes, and an apple butter ham sandwich."

He released a happy sigh. "My favorite."

Officer Maeson sat silent for a while as if trying to decide whether accepting her offer was against policy or not. Then a hint of a smile touched his lips. "Yes, I'd appreciate that."

Cheryl had just returned to her seat when another officer approached. He was the one who had been talking to Levi at the church.

"Ma'am, if you could follow me back, you can see your husband now."

Cheryl read his name tag. "Yes, Officer Abel." She followed him, butterflies dancing in her stomach. She used to get butterflies the first few years of knowing Levi. The sight of his handsome face and his tender, caring attitude had drawn her to him. But now, these were different fluttering emotions. Her love for him made her nervous about what was going to happen. Did the police really think he had something to do with the accident? Obviously, they must.

Officer Abel led her down a hall, and then he stopped in front of a door with a small window. Cheryl paused and peered into the room where Levi sat. His shoulders slumped forward. He looked at his feet, and it seemed like he carried the weight of the world on his shoulders.

"You can go in, ma'am. I'll wait in the other room."

She took a deep breath and walked in slowly. Levi raised his head, and when he saw her, his eyes brightened. Then, just as quickly, worry filled his face. Cheryl rushed to him. "Levi, are you okay?"

"I—I guess I am. I am so sorry, Cheryl. I do not know what is happening. Did they talk to you? Did they say how Rudy is doing?" He released a heavy sigh. "I saw what happened, and it was just plain awful. I—I cannot get the sound of his body hitting the ground out of my mind." Levi lowered his head again.

Beads of sweat dotted his forehead, and Cheryl noticed that it was extremely warm in the room. She fanned her face and then removed her coat. Levi's coat. She laid it on the table then sat down beside him.

Levi lifted one eyebrow. "I did not know that dirty work jackets were the new style."

She tried to smile, but her lower lip quivered. "I put it on to shovel the steps and then grabbed it before we came to town, since it was on top."

Cheryl reached forward and took his hand. Her hand seemed so small in his larger one. She squeezed, attempting to offer him strength. "I don't know anything about how Rudy's doing. I haven't heard anything. The ambulance took him away. But Levi, surely they don't think you had anything to do with this."

"They said they just wanted to take me in for questioning. I guess it is because I built the set and the platform. Something was very wrong. Someone must have messed with it. Rudy had just gotten up there when the platform tipped. It was as if someone released a lever and the whole thing dumped over. I cannot make sense of it."

Cheryl stroked the back of Levi's hand with her thumb and bit her lip. She'd hardly seen him lately, but when they were together, she'd noticed that he was weary to the bone. Perhaps he'd hurried to finish the job and hadn't given the construction the attention he should have. She hated to think it was possible.

Still, she wondered how she could ask about it without hurting him. She released the breath she'd been holding. She knew it was the same question the police had already asked him, but she had to know. "Do you know for certain the platform was secure? It was such a large set. So many pieces—"

"*Ja*." The word shot from his lips, and he leveled a gaze at her. Cheryl pulled back, surprised by his reaction.

"Ja, I know it was secure. But they are saying it is my fault. They are saying I did not secure the platform well enough, but I know I did. That is what took so long last night. That is why I was not home until late, and I was up and out the door early this morning. I wanted to make sure *everything* was secure."

"Yes, yes. I'm sorry I asked. I know you. I know your work. You never leave anything unfinished. You double-check everything." As she spoke the words, Cheryl realized that their conversation was probably being listened to and maybe even recorded.

She squeezed her husband's hand again. It was always important for her to be a caring wife but now even more so. "Listen, it'll all work out. I know you didn't do this. I know you didn't do anything wrong."

Levi released a heavy breath. "That is good to know. I was worried. But still…they said I cannot go home yet. I have to stay one night at least but probably more. Between the fight I had with Rudy just before and the fact I built the set… Well, they said they cannot let me go."

Cheryl leaned in close. "What was that fight about? It sounded like Rudy was very angry."

"I was trying to get him to calm down. I told him we could talk about the problem with the property another time." He sighed. "I feel horrible, Cheryl. I have not been around much, and I know things are hard with the kids."

"You don't have to worry about me, Levi. And you don't have to worry about the kids. I'm going to figure this out."

Levi frowned. "You do not need to get in the middle of this. If someone did try to hurt Rudy, then I do not want you involved in any way."

She waved her hand in the air as if waving off his concern. "I'm not going to get in any trouble. I'm just going to ask around."

"You and my mother, you have been up to this for so long…." A smile lit his face. "I know what it is like when you start asking questions."

Looking at her husband, Cheryl saw that he battled between worry about the accident and concern for her, but mostly she saw his love. A hint of joy filled her heart. They had faced so many things before getting married, and she knew that, as hard as the upcoming days might be, they were in this together. And even though Levi told her not to get involved, there was also a deep trust within her husband's gaze. He knew she wouldn't let this go. He knew she would do everything she could to find answers.

"Cheryl, how are the kids? How is Rebecca?" Her husband's voice interrupted her thoughts. "Did she see what happened?"

"She saw him fall and heard the crash. She was frightened, but she'll be okay. She's with your parents and Esther. Your *daed* and *maam* were in town picking up Esther from work when they heard what happened, and they offered to take the kids home with them so I could figure out what was happening with you."

"Does Rebecca know where I am?" Levi's face was full of concern.

"She doesn't know you're here. I told her that you had to help the police find out what happened."

Levi nodded. "Well, I guess that is true."

"Levi, it's going to be okay."

The words were barely out of Cheryl's mouth when the door opened and Officer Abel entered. "Mrs. Miller, I can walk you out."

Panic rose in Cheryl's chest at the thought of leaving without Levi. "Wait. Are you sending me home without my husband? There's nothing else we can do? I don't like the idea of him having to stay here." The words came out in a flurry. "You have to charge him before you keep him, don't you?"

Officer Abel cleared his throat and puffed out his chest. From his narrowed gaze Cheryl could tell he wasn't happy with her questions. "Ma'am, we can hold a suspect for seventy-two hours without charges. A serious accident happened today on the structure your husband built, injuring a man several witnesses saw your husband arguing with. More than that, screws were missing from the platform, and your husband confessed that he did not see another person touch that platform—today or any other day. We have decided to hold him. I'm sure you understand."

She glanced at Levi, her heartbeat quickening. To her amazement, instead of stress or worry, she saw only resignation in his gaze.

"I will be all right, Cheryl. You will see."

She forced a smile. "You're going to be getting out of here soon, and we're going to have Christmas. We're going to have an extra-special Christmas. I'm praying for that. That's what we have to lean on. We have to pray. I know God has not abandoned us. He's going to help us. He's going to help you. Levi, God's going to help you stay strong, and He's going to help us have Christmas together."

She reached for his coat and picked it up, her eyes still focused on his. Suddenly she heard clattering and looked to see that the contents of Levi's jacket pockets were now on the floor. Bits of twine, old lug nuts, a measuring tape, and screws.

Cheryl moaned. "Look what I did now."

Levi bent to help her pick the things up, but a shout from the officer caused both of them to freeze. "No! Stop!"

Officer Abel pointed to the coat she still held. "Whose coat is that?"

"It's Levi's. I grabbed it as I was racing out the door and wore it to town by accident."

The officer turned to look at Levi. "And when was the last time you wore this jacket?"

Levi's eyes widened. He looked from the officer to Cheryl, to the things spilled onto the ground, and then back up at Cheryl. "Uh, last night. I took it off and hung it on the coatrack when I got home last night."

The officer pulled a handkerchief from his pocket. Then, gingerly, he bent down and picked up one of the screws. "This is a problem then, isn't it, sir? We are looking for missing screws, and you have supplied them." He straightened up and looked at Cheryl. "Your husband will not be leaving here anytime soon, Mrs. Miller."

CHAPTER FIVE

So many things filled Cheryl's mind as she drove to Seth and Naomi's house. Levi didn't have a chance to tell her much about the fight with Rudy. After Officer Abel gathered the screws for evidence, another officer told Cheryl that her time was up and she'd have to return tomorrow.

She told herself to try to relax so the kids wouldn't pick up on her worry. Still, it was hard. Naomi noticed it right away. Rebecca, so much like her grandmother, did too. As Cheryl entered, both of them looked at her with deep concern on their faces.

Even though Christmas was less than two weeks away, there were not many decorations in the Miller kitchen. There was no tree, no ornaments. There were no Christmas villages or nativity scenes. Instead, a simple pine wreath hung over the mantel, brightening the room. Esther must have purchased one from the Swiss Miss.

Rebecca was wearing a new T-shirt. WILD AS MY CURLS, it read. Cheryl guessed that Auntie Elizabeth picked it up for her somewhere. Elizabeth noted both traits about Rebecca often. Cheryl gave Rebecca a quick hug.

Naomi rushed forward and placed a hand on Cheryl's arm. Finally feeling like she was in a safe place, Cheryl nearly collapsed onto a kitchen chair. "He has to stay there." The words were no more than a whisper, but she could barely get them out.

Naomi nodded her understanding, sadness filling her eyes. She placed her fingertips on her lips as if willing herself to stay calm.

"Mommy, were you crying?" Rebecca sat in the chair next to her and touched Cheryl's cheek.

"A little." Cheryl pressed her lips together. "But sometimes it's okay to be sad."

Rebecca twirled one of her curls around her finger. "Oma and I prayed for Mr. Rudy. Oma said we should pray for Daddy too."

Cheryl nodded. "That's a good idea."

Rebecca placed a hand on her hip. "But Matthew didn't want to pray. He wanted to go see the goats instead."

Cheryl couldn't help but chuckle at that. "I was wondering why it was so quiet in here. I bet Matthew, Opa, and the goats are having a wonderful time." She winked at Rebecca. "That's okay about Matthew wanting to see the goats. Your brother is still learning. Someday, he'll be big like you and understand more."

Naomi rose and put the teakettle on. When it whistled, she fixed mugs of peppermint tea for them both. Cheryl wanted nothing more than just to curl up on the couch and nap for a while. The weariness of the day made her eyelids heavy. But lying down even for a minute wasn't an option. She still had a sensitive little girl and an active boy who needed her. She had to find a way to be there for her children and also help Levi. The kids needed their daddy home.

Naomi got up to check on her bread in the oven. Rebecca hurried away to find her boots to go to the barn and let Matthew know it was time to go. And, as she sipped her tea, Cheryl was already making a list of questions. Things she would ponder after she got her kids in bed.

Why were Levi and Rudy arguing? They had been next-door neighbors for years, and they always seemed to get along well. They weren't the best of friends, but they weren't enemies either. Also, it was strange that Sarah and Joe had shown up at today's event and then later at her house, if they were the ones Judith had seen. No one had heard much from them in years, and now they showed up twice in one day. And what were they doing talking to Owen Wight?

Sarah had mentioned that they were looking at property in and around Sugarcreek. Was it the Wight property? Cheryl was pretty sure it had been for sale, but she didn't know what happened with that. Perhaps she could search for the address. Maybe an old real estate listing would show up. And if someone was trying to hurt Rudy, did it have anything to do with the property? Levi had even mentioned that the property was the reason for their argument. Cheryl didn't know her neighbors very well. It would be good to ask about them around town. Maybe folks who knew Rudy and his wife better would have some ideas of who would want to hurt him.

Then Cheryl thought of something that had happened a month or so earlier. Like a foggy memory, it came back. Levi had gone over to talk to Rudy. He had said there was a problem, and he just wanted to clear the air. She remembered trying to listen as Levi explained the issue with the neighbor, but she was in the middle of cooking dinner, the kids were yelling in the next room, and she hadn't been sleeping well. The whole conversation was just a blur.

A few days later, they'd been invited to go over to Seth and Naomi's for a bonfire with s'mores, and Levi had told her that he and Rudy were still trying to work things out. Or maybe he had said he was still trying to get a hold of Rudy to work things out. She hadn't asked too many questions. She'd just figured that, in Levi's unassuming way, he would be able to go over, talk to the neighbor, and resolve everything. Obviously, that hadn't happened, and she felt horrible for not paying better attention.

What had been going on had most likely been bothering Levi for a while, so maybe it was more than just a hectic life that was causing him to be quieter than usual. If so, Cheryl knew she was partly to blame. She'd been so busy lately with the kids, serving in the church, and helping Esther get everything ready for the Christmas-shopping season at the Swiss Miss. She realized now that all her busyness hadn't left time or energy for one of the most important parts of her life—her relationship with Levi.

When Cheryl had first come to Sugarcreek to manage the Swiss Miss gift shop for Aunt Mitzi, she'd never dreamed of all the good gifts God had waiting for her. First, her friendship with Naomi. Then her marriage to Levi and the arrival of their children. These were things she hadn't dared to dream about during her corporate banking days. Yet recently, she'd been too busy to truly pay attention to what was going on with the person she loved most.

Once or twice, Cheryl had suggested to Levi that they should go out on a date night, but she had never sat down and made plans. Yes, he'd been busy, but perhaps she could have packed hot cocoa and joined him—if only for an hour. She hadn't made it happen, and she hadn't paused long enough to listen to Levi— to understand his heart, to discuss his problems—and now this. Would he be willing to open up and talk to her about it? She hoped so, even though she hadn't taken time to listen to him sooner.

Naomi approached with her own cup of tea and took a seat at the table. "Deep in thought, I see."

"Yes, there are so many things to think about. The police are convinced that someone intentionally sabotaged the platform to hurt Rudy. Since I know it wasn't Levi, I was trying to think of who would do such a thing and why. Unfortunately, I don't know Rudy well enough to come up with any ideas. Also, Levi did mention to me awhile back that there was some type of conflict happening between him and Rudy. I wish I had paid closer attention. It seems as if every conversation we have is interrupted by the kids, and that one was no exception."

Naomi reached across the table and patted Cheryl's hand. "These are the busiest of all parenting years, to be sure. As wonderful as children are, they are exhausting and demanding. And did I say exhausting?" Naomi laughed.

Cheryl smiled at her joke. "I'm sure you handled things so much better. Your house seems to run like a well-oiled machine. It's always so clean and peaceful."

"Oh dear, Cheryl. You should have seen it when the children were young. I was an instant mother to three children when I was only twenty years old, remember? And they had lived without a mother for many years. The children ruled the roost for quite a while, even though I tried to do my best. One thing you cannot do is compare someone else's end, or even middle, to your beginning."

"So are you saying that things haven't always been perfectly easy for you?"

"Not even close. Give yourself grace. You are doing a wonderful job as a mother, and Levi loves you deeply. I see the way he looks at you, Cheryl, when he does not think anyone is looking."

Tears welled up again in Cheryl's eyes.

Naomi wrapped her hands around her mug. "I know, and Levi knows, that you will do all you can to help him. You are a smart woman. You have proven that time and time again."

Cheryl took a deep breath and then let it out slowly. It helped to know that others didn't think she was utterly failing in her role as a wife and mother even though it felt that way sometimes.

Naomi offered for the kids to stay the night, but Cheryl declined. Even though it would be easier for her if they weren't underfoot this evening, she didn't want to go back to an empty house. She'd had many years when it was just her and Beau. Tonight, she wanted her kids near. Still, that didn't mean it would be easy.

"Naomi, I don't know what we're going to do. My heart hurts so much knowing that Levi will be sleeping in that jail tonight. And what am I going to tell the children?"

Naomi sighed. "Remember that saying, 'We move forward, into the future, one day at a time'? The good news is we do not have to figure everything out at this moment. Levi will be all right. He is not alone, Cheryl. God is with him. And with you too. God is going to be with you tonight."

Naomi spoke with such faith and confidence that a gentle peace floated over Cheryl's soul. Yes, she still had many questions, but it helped to be reminded that God had answers. It was good to talk to Naomi, to glean from her wisdom. As much as Cheryl loved her parents, she didn't have the same heart connection with them so far away, as she did with Naomi. Naomi had been a dear friend even before she became her mother-in-law, and being a good friend was one of the things that Naomi did best.

"Seth and I already talked to the children," Naomi added, stirring honey into her tea. "We told them that the police just needed to talk to their daed for a while. We said that everyone is praying to ask that God makes Mr. Rudy feel better. We also told them that their daed might not be able to sleep at home tonight. They seemed to understand."

Cheryl reached for Naomi and gave her a quick hug. "Thank you. I'm so glad you knew what to say. Being a parent is not the easiest thing in the world."

"No, but you are doing a wonderful job. Just wonderful. The children have a good, happy life. They have two caring parents who love them. And we can trust that God is going to be with us this Christmas. He will make sure that everything will work out for our good."

Cheryl replayed the words in her mind. *He will make sure that everything will work out for our good.* She also sent up a silent prayer that she could truly believe that. Levi needed her to stay strong. She wouldn't be able to help him if she fell apart.

Seth entered the house with the two kids, both talking at once, telling her about the goats. They talked all the way home too, and Cheryl didn't mind. She needed life to feel normal, or as normal as it could.

Cheryl lay in bed that night, shivering beneath the sheets. She turned to one side and then the other. Her worried, racing thoughts chased away sleep, much to her dismay.

The space next to her felt cold, and she missed Levi's warmth and soft breathing. She tried to imagine where he slept tonight—a cold bunk, maybe even without a pillow or blanket. No, that wasn't right. Surely he'd have a blanket. She shivered again thinking of the cement walls and iron bars locking him in. Did he have to share the cell with another person?

She and Levi hadn't spent much time apart in their years of marriage. From the time she said, "I do," Cheryl was content to spend every day and night with Levi at her side. *No, I can't think of where he is. I need sleep, and I need happy memories and hope.*

Trying to push away the dark, foreboding thoughts, Cheryl thought back to their wedding at the Miller farm. It had been an outdoor ceremony, and there were a lot of Amish and Mennonites there. The Mennonite minister and Cheryl's dad both had parts in the ceremony. She snuggled into her pillow and smiled, remembering that her brother Matt and Aunt Mitzi had surprised them by being there.

She'd worn a simple white dress with lace and cap sleeves. The Amish women provided the food, and the Mennonite women did the decorating, including creating table arrangements with mason jars and an abundance of colorful flowers. It brought her joy to remember that day, but also a longing too.

As wonderful as it was to get a box from Aunt Mitzi, Cheryl wished her aunt would somehow surprise her on the front doorstep with her presence. She knew that Aunt Mitzi would have wise words to buoy her soul.

And what would happen if Levi was actually put under arrest and had to spend Christmas in jail? What if she couldn't prove that he was innocent before that? Or ever? A small knot of worry in her stomach tightened as the minutes ticked by. Even though she had promised Rebecca that they could make Christmas cookies the next day, Cheryl knew she needed to ask Elizabeth or Esther to babysit the kids. Rebecca would be disappointed about not making cookies together, but the greatest gift Cheryl could give her daughter and her son this Christmas was to make sure that their father came home.

Cheryl tossed and turned. The police had said it was clear that someone had removed the screws from the platform. The holes were drilled, but the screws weren't there. But who would do that? Who would want to hurt Rudy?

The first name that popped into Cheryl's mind was Owen, Rudy's son. Something about his actions that day were odd. He was there when his father was hurt, yet instead of running to see if he was okay, Owen ran for the police officer. And even after he alerted law enforcement, he ran in Levi's direction instead of checking on his father. Wouldn't a son be more concerned about seeing that his father was okay? And why would Owen be so set on accusing Levi? Was he upset by the shouting match between Rudy and Levi right before the presentation was due to start?

In all her days of sleuthing with Naomi, Cheryl had learned to not only think of who could have done something but also why they would do it. She knew enough about her neighbors to know that Owen was their only child, so he could very well be heir to his father's property. Or would Rudy's wife inherit it? If Rudy died, would Owen have more say over the property and be free to sell it? It would have to be someone very heartless to think about injuring his own father for the sake of a piece of property or the money it could bring from its sale. Then again, there could be a host of other reasons why a son would want to hurt his father and not just for an inheritance.

Unable to sleep, Cheryl got up and decided to do some cleaning. Dinner dishes were still in the sink, and toys littered the living room floor. Then there was the toothpaste smeared into the bathroom floor and sink. It would take extra scrubbing since the toothpaste had dried.

It took less than thirty minutes for Cheryl to load the dishwasher, clean the bathroom, and get all the toys into the toy box. She picked up the empty box from Aunt Mitzi to put it into the recycle bin when she noticed something at the bottom. There was an envelope with her name written on it. How had she missed this? With eager fingers, Cheryl opened the envelope and pulled out a letter.

My Darling Cheryl,

No doubt, by the time you get this, winter will have settled over the farm. As much as I love Ohio, I do not miss shoveling snow or driving on ice. I don't miss the long, dark days or feeling cut off from friends.

As I was praying for you, I felt drawn to pray for your peace. Lately, your letters and emails have shared a lot about what the kids are doing and what Levi is up to, yet I've heard little of how you're doing—how you're really doing.

It's so easy to get caught up in our roles, isn't it, that we forget to be people. I hope you're taking some time for yourself. Maybe consider having lunch with a friend or sitting down to read another chapter in a favorite novel, even if there are dishes in the sink. Also, I want to encourage you to take time to sit before God and ask Him who you can be a blessing to on that day. This advice may seem the opposite of taking time for yourself, but it's not. When you allow God's love to pour through you to others, you get to partake of the blessing too. Isn't that beautiful? So, if God brings a person to mind, that's His invitation for you to reach out. It's always the right time to do the right thing. This is why I included a present for Sarah and her husband, Joe. Lately, every time I pray for Levi's family, Sarah's name comes to mind. I'm not sure if you even see her or talk to her much, but if you could find a way to deliver these packages to her, I would be most appreciative. Maybe Sarah just needs a little reminder that God loves her, don't you think?

I must sign off now, but remember that God will be with you through every storm. The winds may howl, but He holds the winds in His hands. You can count on that.

Love, Aunt Mitzi

Cheryl read the letter twice and then sat there in disbelief. Aunt Mitzi had done it again—said just the thing she needed to hear right when she needed to hear it. Or actually, God had done it again. He'd directed Aunt Mitzi to write those words to her and also to buy gifts for Sarah and Joe. How amazing that today, of all days, the package would come. And just knowing that God made all this possible brought another measure of peace. Finally, with Aunt Mitzi's message floating through her mind, Cheryl was able to climb back into bed and drift off to sleep.

CHAPTER SIX

Cheryl hurried toward her car. The crisp air wrapped around her in a nippy breeze. A few dead leaves danced across the snow as if leading the way. She shivered and rubbed her hands together as she walked. Thankfully, Elizabeth had taken it upon herself to come over bright and early to help with Rebecca and Matthew. She had shown up with all the ingredients for gingerbread, plus the frosting, candy canes, and gumdrops for the gingerbread houses they were going to make. With all those treats laid out before them, the kids didn't seem to mind when Cheryl told them she needed to go to town for most of the day. This would give her a chance to figure some things out. She had to get some answers for Levi's sake.

As she drove toward Sugarcreek, snowy branches hung above her head like outstretched arms over the roadway. What had Rebecca called it? Their white-sparkle tunnel. It seemed fitting. Cheryl smiled at the thought of her Mini-Me. Rebecca's auburn hair was so similar to hers when she was that age. Rebecca looked very much like Cheryl, but the older her daughter got, Cheryl also realized she had her dad's gentle nature. She was also full of questions. Did Levi have so many questions inside him? If he did, he only picked a few, every once in a while, to ask.

Cheryl's heart also welled to think of Matthew. His name meant "gift from God," and he truly was a gift to their family. Although he didn't look like either her or Levi, she sometimes noticed little things he did that reminded her of both of them. He often scratched his head when he had a question, just like Levi did. He also had a habit of walking around and mumbling to himself, just like Cheryl found herself doing at times.

Turning onto the main highway and passing an older couple in a buggy, Cheryl remembered the days when Levi had driven her around in his horse and buggy. It had been so wonderful to be with him. He had led her to a slower pace of life that she had never known and one that she enjoyed. But instead of remaining there, she somehow got Levi to hurry things up. When had that happened? It pinched her heart to think of that.

Cheryl turned off Highway 39 in front of the Swiss Miss, and she saw that the front display window of the gift shop looked perfectly inviting. The small building, painted a cream color with cornflower-blue accents and red shutters, was always welcoming, but at Christmas it looked downright festive.

Cheryl walked up the sidewalk and paused for a moment under the red-and-white-striped awning. Red and silver ornaments swung from green garland gracing the window. The cold wind nipped at Cheryl's nose, and she tucked her scarf tighter under her chin. She urged herself to stay strong. That was the only way she'd make it through the day.

Both Lydia and Esther were scheduled to work on what was sure to be a busy morning. Holiday shopping had begun in earnest with out-of-town visitors coming for Christmas in the Village, an all-day celebration culminating with a candle lighting ceremony that would recognize one of the town's unsung heroes. The drive-by live nativity was supposed to be an additional attraction, but now that wouldn't happen. All that work for nothing. Or, even worse, after all that work, Levi's reward was him sitting inside a holding cell at the Sugarcreek Police Department.

When she stepped into the shop, Esther was there to greet her. She must have seen Cheryl as she paused outside. The younger woman wrapped Cheryl in a warm embrace. "Are you all right? I heard about everything that happened."

Cheryl opened her mouth to say she was fine, but words wouldn't come. Instead, she just nodded.

In the far corner of the store, Lydia was helping a man look through boxes of Christmas cards. He had light brown hair and wore wire-rimmed glasses. Cheryl didn't think much about him until she looked again and saw him staring at her. When she peeked once more and made eye contact with him, he quickly averted his gaze.

Cheryl turned her back to him and lifted both eyebrows to get Esther's attention.

"What is it, Cheryl? Is there a problem?" Esther's voice rose in alarm.

So much for being subtle.

"Esther..." Cheryl spoke between clenched teeth. "Do you happen to know who that man is?"

"*Ne.* He was here first thing this morning, and he has been looking at everything in the store. But I have not seen him before. Perhaps he is from out of town?"

"Yes, perhaps." Cheryl forced a smile. "I thought he was watching me, but I might just be imagining things. After yesterday I'm a bit on edge." Cheryl took a deep breath and composed herself. She refused to look at the man again and guessed it was just her nerves getting the best of her. She moved toward her office.

Esther called out. "Oh, Cheryl."

"Yes?" She paused. As she scanned the store, Cheryl saw that the man was gone. Again, she pushed her concern out of her mind. *It's nothing. He was just another tourist,* she scolded herself.

"Cheryl, Daed called," Esther said in her singsong voice. "He said not to worry about doing the chores. He is going over to take care of them. He said he tried to call your phone, but you did not answer. My guess is that he called your house phone but didn't think to call your cell phone. Anyway, he called here to let me know just in case you stopped by."

Cheryl pressed a hand to her forehead. Even though she'd thought about a thousand things last night, she hadn't thought about the chores once.

"Oh yes, wonderful. Tell your daed thank you from me when you see him. I surely appreciate that."

Levi always took care of the animals. He made sure there was wood for the fire. Even though he had only started driving in recent years, he also checked to make sure Cheryl never had less than half a tank of gas in her vehicle. What would she do without him around? She had been used to living alone for so many years, but now she was used to just the opposite. She had come to depend on Levi for so many things. Thankfully, his father had stepped in. But if they couldn't find the answers they needed to clear Levi's name, would Seth always be able to come to her aid? Most likely not.

"No, no, no," Cheryl whispered as she pushed those thoughts out of her mind. *I can't think of this being a long-term thing. It isn't. It won't be. Levi isn't guilty of any crime.*

Cheryl released the breath she'd been holding, willing her frayed nerves to calm. The bell on the front door jingled. She turned, and her heartbeat quickened to see Naomi walk in, her eyes fixed on Cheryl. When she reached her, she pulled off her red mittens, took Cheryl's hands, and gave them a squeeze. That simple act filled Cheryl's heart with warmth, affirming that her mother-in-law would be there to help her. She would not have to figure everything out alone.

"I knew I would find you here, especially after I heard that both Elizabeth and Seth would be tending to matters at your place today." Naomi squeezed Cheryl's hands again.

"Yes. Elizabeth got a ride from a neighbor this morning, and Esther just told me that Seth was going to our place to do the chores. I assume Seth took the buggy, so how did you get here? You didn't hitchhike, did you?" The thought of Naomi standing along the road with her thumb out brought a smile to Cheryl's face.

"*Ach*, actually, you are not far from the truth. I know that the Yoder boy, who just got married, has been working in town. He passes every morning, and I decided to watch for him and ask for a ride. He didn't seem surprised by my request. Word has gotten out about the accident in the community, and he was glad to help." Naomi clapped her hands together. "Now tell me, how are we going to get started?"

"I just came by to use the computer. There are some things I want to research, and I thought it would be easier to look up information on my office computer than on my phone."

Naomi waved at Esther, who was straightening up a shelf of Amish dolls. "Yes, of course. Know that I am here to help with whatever is needed…" Naomi raised an eyebrow and tucked a stray strand of hair into her *kapp*. "But nothing dangerous, of course."

Cheryl feigned surprise. "No, of course not." She pressed a hand to her forehead. "The first thing I need to do is call an attorney. I can't believe I forgot to talk to Levi about what he wants me to do—who he thinks I should reach out to. I suppose I was just so thankful to see him."

Naomi shook her head and leaned closer. "I guarantee Levi will not want that—you reaching out and finding an attorney."

Cheryl's eyes widened. "What do you mean?"

"We do not believe in working with lawyers or attorneys. Our word is our word. We will not lie, so why should we pay someone to defend the truth?"

"Of course… But we need the help. Levi needs the help. Maybe if I just call—"

Naomi placed a hand on Cheryl's arm. "Perhaps you should talk to Levi first. It would be a waste of your time and money to find someone, especially if it goes against Levi's morals and beliefs."

Why did I marry a man with such morals and beliefs? The words shot through Cheryl's mind, and she nearly laughed at herself for thinking them. Having high standards and morals wasn't a fault. Still, she would talk to Levi about this when she next saw him. Yes, his word was his word, but how would that help if the evidence seemed stacked against him?

Naomi stepped closer again, leaning in near Cheryl's ear, interrupting her thoughts. "Have you heard anything about the man who was hurt?"

"I called the Canton hospital this morning, but since I'm not family they couldn't give me any information. But I'll take the fact that Rudy is still there as a good thing. I'm praying that he makes a full recovery. That accident was so—" Emotion caught in her throat. "So horrible."

Naomi's eyebrows lifted in a worried expression. "Ja, well, I have a feeling that whoever hurt Rudy would not hesitate to do the same to others—even us."

Cheryl knew there was always danger anytime one started asking questions and poking around to find the truth. But finding answers had always been important to her. And with Levi under suspicion, the truth mattered more now than it ever had.

Cheryl removed her coat and ran her fingers through her hair where her hood had pressed it down. Then she motioned toward her office, welcoming Naomi to join her. "I'm glad you're here. I didn't realize how much I needed someone by my side through all this until I saw you walk through that door."

Naomi smiled. "It is all right to need someone, but I will leave those searches on the computer to you." She winked.

Side by side, they walked past the display cases filled with all types of merchandise. Esther had done a great job adding LED candles and greenery to the shelves, giving them all a festive glow. Although she could do little decorating at her parents' home, she made up for it here.

Once she'd logged on to her computer, Cheryl's first order of business was to see if Rudy Wight's property had recently been put up for sale. She put in the address and did a web search. Naomi leaned in close, looking at the screen with curiosity.

Within thirty seconds, Cheryl had her answer. "Look here." She pointed to the photo on the screen. "Rudy's house was listed for sale three months ago." She scrolled through the photos of the property.

"Such a pretty place," Naomi commented. "We have passed by the farm so often, just seeing it from the road. It is nice to see it up close."

It was beautiful indeed, with a large pasture area, a sprawling house, a well-built barn, and a row of tall trees leading down the driveway to the property. Then Cheryl looked at the sale price, and her stomach flipped.

She pointed to the screen. "Do you see the price? Can that be right?"

Naomi let out a low whistle. "It is far more than I expected."

"I suppose we shouldn't be surprised. I guess all sorts of people would love to move onto such a beautiful farm in the middle of Amish Country. I know I did."

The page also showed that the property had been taken off the market. Cheryl wondered why. She looked at the Realtor's name and jotted it down.

"I recognize this name, and the Realtor's office is just a few blocks away." She turned to Naomi. "We should head over and talk to him. I still have a couple of hours before I can visit Levi. Maybe before then we can get an answer as to why the property was taken off the market. And whether the high price on that farm has anything to do with Rudy's accident."

Chapter Seven

With Naomi by her side, Cheryl had only walked a few blocks when something caught her attention. The large barnlike structure was still erected on the front lawn of Community Bible Church. The manger and bales of hay were still displayed inside, but instead of appearing as a joyous part of the Sugarcreek holiday scene, the whole set was a stark reminder of what had happened the day before.

As hard as it was seeing the empty structure, worse was seeing the yellow tape that had been strung up, letting people know it was still considered a crime scene. A man walked around with a notebook in his hand and a camera hung around his neck. From the way he was observing the area, Cheryl guessed he was some type of law enforcement officer. She slowed her steps, and Naomi did the same.

"Do you want to talk to him?" Naomi asked.

Cheryl bit her lip. "Do you think he'd mind if we went over there?"

"Well, he probably would mind if we both went over," Naomi said. "Why don't you go alone? Then it would not seem so intrusive." She motioned down the street. "I still have a few gifts to buy, and I would be happy to window shop. Then I will join you again when you head to Sugarcreek Realty."

"That's a good idea. I'll let you know if I learn anything."

"Wonderful, and I will let you know if I spot any good sales." Naomi continued down the sidewalk.

After she had moved to Sugarcreek, Cheryl found herself caught up in numerous mysteries. She'd worked with law enforcement far more than she'd ever imagined she would, so she walked toward the man with confident steps. But more than that, she walked with a prayer on her lips. This time it was personal. Whatever the man concluded might directly impact her husband's future, her future.

The man looked up at her when she approached. She recognized his dark hair with gray at the temples and his kind blue eyes.

"Carlos?" she called out to him. "Is that you?" Carlos Diaz had attended church with her for years before Cheryl had started attending Friendship Mennonite Church, and for a moment Cheryl wondered if he was simply a curious church member.

"Yes, and I can read the questions in your gaze. Unfortunately, I'm here on official business."

Cheryl paused at the edge of the yellow tape. She lifted her eyebrows. "Is that so?"

"Actually, yes." Carlos reached his hand into his interior jacket pocket and pulled out a badge. "I'm a state detective now. I mostly work in Berlin, but since this is my community and I'm familiar with the folks involved, they put me on the case." He put his badge back in his pocket. "My gut tells me that Levi wasn't involved in this accident, regardless of what it looks like, but I still have to follow the evidence."

Cheryl crossed her arms over her thick coat. "So would you mind if I hung around to watch you?"

Carlos shrugged. "I probably shouldn't let you, but since I know you…" He winked at Cheryl.

He stepped closer to the wooden platform. It lay at an awkward angle on the ground where it had fallen. The snow around the area had been trampled down. The wood was cracked, splintered from Rudy Wight's weight. Seeing that, Cheryl swallowed her emotion.

Carlos took a pencil from his shirt pocket and pointed to the platform. "I can see here that the holes were drilled. Levi said he drilled the screws directly in."

"So that means Levi was telling the truth when he said he secured the platform." Hope pounded in Cheryl's chest.

"I wish it were that easy." He shook his head.

"So taking Levi's word for it isn't good enough, even though the holes are proof that he screwed them?"

"Unfortunately not. A prosecuting attorney would claim that either Levi was negligent or that the incident was premeditated. The holes mean nothing. The screws were not present when Rudy Wight stepped on the platform. That is the one thing we do know." He leaned closer, taking a better look. Concern clouded his face.

"And I can see there's more you're not telling me."

"I really shouldn't be telling you anything, Cheryl, but there are a lot of problems here. To be honest, it's not going to be easy for anyone to prove Levi's innocence. Not only did Levi have the ability to create an unstable environment that was sure to bring

Rudy to the ground, but from what some of our witnesses say, he also had motive." Carlos straightened, focusing on her face. Sadness filled his gaze.

"Are you talking about the argument between Levi and Rudy right before the beginning of the program? I witnessed it, and many others did too, but surely they would have noticed that Levi was trying not to make a scene. In fact, he was trying to calm Rudy down."

"If it was just that, it wouldn't be so bad. But I've heard that some people close to the situation have already testified that there was bad blood between Levi and Rudy."

Owen. The young man's face filled Cheryl's mind. By the way he had acted yesterday, accusing Levi from the moment his father fell, there was no doubt it was him.

"Does this person happen to be related to Rudy?" she dared to ask.

"I can't say much, and I can't name names, but from what I hear, it was a feud, and not a little one at that." He looked at her with raised eyebrows. "Of course, if you have anything to say about that you might want to make an official statement to the police."

"Are you telling me that I shouldn't talk—or at least not without a lawyer? What if I'm not aware of a huge problem between them? Levi said they had some things they needed to talk through, but…" She closed her mouth, pressing her lips tight. Carlos was probably right. A lawyer would be a good idea if she was going to talk at all. The truth was, she didn't know what the big conflict between Levi and Rudy was, even though she was Levi's wife. A prosecuting attorney would have a heyday with that fact. It wouldn't help Levi's case at all. It could be used to try to prove he had something to hide.

Carlos shook his head slowly. It was a warning, she supposed. Carlos was trying to help her by reminding her to be cautious of what she said to whom.

"I'm here to investigate the crime scene, not to interview witnesses. My report will be about what I saw when I studied this structure. It won't say anything about who just happened to be walking to and from the church."

"Thank you," she said. "I guess I do need to be careful what I say."

"And you might need to seek counsel, just in case you're called in for questioning. So far, no one has mentioned that they believe you are involved, but you never know what ideas will pop into people's heads."

"But I don't know anything." Her words came out in a rush, and she felt her defenses rising. "This whole thing has caught me completely off guard. I haven't done anything wrong, just as my husband hasn't done anything wrong. Our kids need both of us to be home, with them."

Carlos shook his head again. "Sadly, Cheryl, that's what they all say."

Cheryl's knees weakened, and she took two steps and leaned against the tall pine tree still decorated with red ornaments. She closed her eyes and told herself to stay calm. In just a few hours, she would be able to see Levi. Maybe she'd get to the station and they'd tell her that this whole thing was just a misunderstanding. Perhaps they'd let Levi go today. She breathed a prayer that it would be so. That hope helped her slow her breathing. She took deep, cleansing breaths and willed herself to calm.

When she opened her eyes, she expected Carlos to be looking at her, watching her have a nervous breakdown. But instead he'd given her space, and he was near the platform taking photos.

As she stood there, Cheryl thought of something else. *Levi's truck.* She turned and scanned the parking lot. Even though she knew Levi had driven his truck to the church yesterday, it wasn't there.

"What happened to Levi's truck?" She spoke more to herself than Carlos.

"I'm sorry, Cheryl. I'm surprised they didn't tell you. They took it in for evidence."

"What do you mean, 'for evidence'? Don't they need a warrant for that?"

"Actually, no. If the police believe it contains evidence connected to the case, they can seize it. But from what I heard, Levi made it easy for them."

"How did he do that?"

"He signed a Consent to Search form."

"So he gave them permission to search his truck?" Cheryl rubbed her forehead. "Yes, of course he did. He knows he's innocent." She released a sigh. How could she fault Levi for being so trustworthy? She just hoped it wouldn't hurt him in the end.

"Of course they would think his truck would have evidence," she mumbled to herself. "But I'm sure they're not going to find anything," she said louder.

"Or, hopefully, Levi will have an explanation for what they *did* find." Carlos jotted more notes in his notebook.

What could they have found? She was afraid to ask. And she was certain Carlos couldn't tell her even if she did ask.

Cheryl suddenly felt numb. It was more than the cold air that was chilling her to the bone. So far, all the news appeared to be bad news. Instead of her finding answers and things getting better, they were getting worse. Cheryl moved away from the tree, looking back over her shoulder at Carlos. "Yes, well, it was good talking to you. Thank you…" She paused, wondering what she could thank him for. Then she had it. "Thank you for believing that Levi did not purposefully or accidentally hurt Rudy Wight. And thank you for doing your job well."

She hoped that sounded neutral. The last thing Cheryl needed was for anyone to think that she was trying to use her friendships for her husband's cause.

"You take care," Carlos called, as if they'd just been talking about the weather instead of Levi's guilt or innocence.

As she walked back in the direction of the Swiss Miss, Cheryl thought about the missing screws that should have been holding the platform together. Yesterday, when the screws fell out of his coat pocket and the officer collected them as evidence, Levi had insisted they were not the ones he'd used on the platform.

Cheryl had confirmed to the officer that Levi indeed kept and reused anything he found useful. She told him that those screws could have been in his pocket for months because she so rarely washed his work jacket.

Unfortunately, the officer hadn't listened. Instead, he took the screws as evidence. Still, he'd been kind enough to let her take the coat home. *Jail my husband, but make sure I make it home warm.* She sighed, wishing she'd been brave enough to say those words. Then again, the officer had only been doing his job. Cheryl had to admit that if she didn't know Levi as well as she did, she'd be giving more weight to all this evidence too.

Chapter Eight

Even though the Realtor's office was right down the street from Community Bible Church, Cheryl no longer had the emotional energy to question anyone. Her mind was already filled with so many worries. She walked with slow steps down the sidewalk, looking into the storefronts for Naomi. Up ahead, a young woman was taking a selfie.

"There are cameras everywhere these days," she mumbled to herself. That's one thing she knew her Amish family members didn't appreciate, since they didn't believe in having their images captured in photographs. Then Cheryl froze in her steps. "There are cameras everywhere!" she said louder.

Cheryl moved back in the direction of the church lawn, scanning the buildings for security cameras. There had to be some around here. Maybe the church even had one.

If there were security cameras, they might have captured the accident. But, more than that, they could have recorded the person who sabotaged the platform sometime between the time Levi left, late in the night, and when he arrived the following morning.

Cheryl hurried in the direction of the street that Naomi had just traveled down, and she found her exiting a thrift store. A small bag hung on her arm.

"Did you find something?" Cheryl said as the door swung closed.

"Not really." Naomi opened the bag to display an array of woolen yarn. "But since socks and mittens disappear one at a time around my place, it is time to stock up to make some more." She took a step closer, and then she turned and pointed to the music shop across the street, closest to the church lawn. "And while I was there earlier, I thought to ask about their security camera. Most businesses have them these days."

Cheryl's eyes widened. "Yes, you're right. In fact, I just thought of the same thing, but I'm surprised…" She let her voice trail off.

"Surprised my mind turned to how something electronic could be of use?" Naomi laughed. "We choose to not allow the world around us to impact our daily lives, Cheryl. But that does not mean we do not know it exists." She clapped her mittened hands together. "Now, what do you think about joining me in talking to the owners of the rest of the shops?"

Cheryl smiled. "Sure, Naomi. I'd be happy to join you."

With eager steps, Cheryl and Naomi stopped at the shops closest to the church. The stores were busy, which was a good thing. While most people told her they would be happy to talk to the police about their security cameras, Cheryl's friends from Swissters seemed especially eager to help. Lisa Troyer took Cheryl and Naomi into her office and listened intently as Naomi explained the reason for their visit. Cheryl looked around the neat office, enjoying the moment to sit and warm up and also humored by her mother-in-law's excitement over cameras, of all things.

"I don't know how to access our cameras, but I'll talk to our security company. I have your number, so if I discover anything I'll let you know." Lisa offered a hopeful smile. "And I'll let the police know too, of course, so they can catch the real criminal."

"Thank you." Naomi sat back in her chair, obviously pleased.

"I really appreciate it," Cheryl said, "but even more I'm thankful that you want to help prove Levi's innocence."

Lisa smiled. "I have a sense about people, and Levi has always given me such a positive impression. I'm just hoping that our camera picked something up. I'm happy to help."

Cheryl's lack of sleep was catching up with her, but she forced herself to rise. There was no time to slow down, especially since Elizabeth was watching the kids, and she had Naomi's assistance too. Cheryl didn't want Levi to stay under police custody one minute longer than he had to. "Thank you again. And don't be surprised if the police come around to ask the same thing. At least I hope they will."

"I have no doubt that they will get around to it, but they better get used to you two being one step ahead of them." Lisa chuckled. "They are certainly no match for a determined wife and mother joined as a team."

"And we have others on our team too. My father-in-law is taking care of the chores. One of my sisters-in-law is watching my children. My other sister-in-law is taking on more responsibilities at the Swiss Miss since I can't be around."

"Well, I'd like to help too. Get yourself a shopping basket, Cheryl, and grab some things to take home. I'm sure you haven't had much time to go grocery shopping."

Cheryl's jaw dropped in surprise. "I haven't, but you don't have to do that."

"I'm offering cheese and crackers, Cheryl. Not a kidney. Get a few things. I'll tell my clerks it's on the house. And know I'll be praying too."

Cheryl picked up a couple of cheese and cracker trays, and then she and Naomi returned to the Swiss Miss. Just a few minutes after they arrived, Seth entered the store. After sharing with Cheryl that he'd fed the animals and finished the chores, he turned to Naomi. "I came to town for more feed and spotted you two from down the street. Do you have time to go to lunch?" As if on cue his stomach growled.

"Well, Seth Miller, is this a date, or did you forget to grab your wallet again?" Naomi winked.

Seth glanced to his feet and shrugged. "Ja, I will admit that is what happened, but we can also call it a date. And thank goodness Sam at the feedstore lets me put everything on a tab to pay at the end of the month."

The banter between her in-laws brought a smile to Cheryl's face until she realized just what Seth had said. It was lunchtime already. "Enjoy your meal, and thank you, Naomi, for your help. I need to get down to the police station. I'm afraid by the time I get there—even if I hurry—I'll miss the first fifteen minutes of visiting time."

Cheryl wrapped her scarf around her neck tighter and then carried her cheese trays to her car. She hoped that when Lisa's security company got access to the tapes there would finally be some proof that Levi was right—that he secured the platform and that it was someone else who'd come and removed the screws in the night.

As she got to her car and slid the grocery bags inside, Cheryl was surprised that two hours had passed since she'd gotten to town. She had just enough time to drive to the police station. Wanting as much time as she could get, she hurried to the door, smoothing her wrinkled clothes and brushing her fingers through tangled hair. She paused at the entrance to the police station and took a deep breath. Thankfully, there wasn't a line, and she hurried to the check-in counter.

Today a female police officer sat at the counter. As Cheryl approached, the officer continued typing on a keyboard and didn't look up.

"My name is Cheryl Miller. I was told I could come for visiting hours. My husband, Levi…" She struggled to get out his name, still in disbelief at the reality of the situation. "My husband, Levi Miller, is here." Cheryl quickly wiped away a tear that refused to be held back.

The police officer glanced up, and the expression on her face softened. She waited as Cheryl composed herself.

"My husband, Levi, is here," Cheryl said again.

"Yes, he is," the officer said gently. "I need to see your ID. A driver's license will work. Then please sign your name on this visitor's list, and I'll have them bring him into the visitation room."

"Yes, of course."

Cheryl filled out all the information and provided her driver's license. Before she could go to the visitation room, she had to leave her coat and purse with the officer and even show that she had nothing in her pockets.

Finally, Cheryl was taken down the hall to a large room. There were already two other people sitting at tables with a visiting family member. Another officer stood near the tables, overseeing their visits.

When Cheryl entered, she looked around the room for Levi, but he wasn't there yet. Anxiety caused a slight ache in her chest, and she ran a finger around her sweater collar, wishing she had fresh air.

The officer standing near her eyed her with concern. "Just take a breath, ma'am. And have a seat. Your husband will be in shortly."

Cheryl nodded. She was surprised that the officer knew she was here visiting her husband. But then again, he probably needed to know information about the prisoners and their visitors. Realizing Levi was in that category caused her to sink lower in the hard plastic chair. This wasn't their life. This wasn't where law-abiding citizens ended up. She knew that most people in here would probably say they were innocent, but Levi truly was.

The door opened, and Levi shuffled in. His clothes were wrinkled and disheveled, and he was unshaven. She rose and, more than anything, wanted to rush forward to him, yet one look at the officer leading Levi told her that wasn't allowed.

"Remember, no physical contact, ma'am," he emphasized.

Remember? she wanted to scream. *How can I remember if we've never done this before?* But instead of commenting, Cheryl sat and waited for Levi to do the same.

By this time, there was only thirty minutes left to their visit, and she didn't want to waste it in small talk.

"Levi, why do they think you would want to hurt Rudy?"

Levi didn't appear surprised by the question. The tense look on his face softened. "I can tell you are a woman on a mission. I will wait until later to ask you to give the children hugs from me." He chuckled, and then his voice lowered. "I know I mentioned it before, but I did not want to go into too many details about the problems between us—Rudy and me."

"They must be pretty serious for the police to think you'd want to hurt him," she said, softening her voice so that Levi didn't think that she was interrogating him too.

"It started when I cut off limbs on a row of trees that hung over the property line. I tried to talk to Rudy before I did it, but I could not get a hold of him. I guess that made him pretty mad. There are things I need to talk to you about, Cheryl, when we have time."

"I understand if this isn't the right time or the right place, but what happened yesterday, Levi? What was the shouting about? I could hardly sleep last night thinking about it."

Levi paused. "Yesterday was the first time I had seen Rudy face-to-face in months. And when he started shouting, well, I did not know how to respond." Levi pressed his hand to his forehead, emotion clear on his face. He looked as if he'd just awakened from a nightmare. But the situation wasn't a bad dream. They were sitting here, in a jail visitation room, talking under the scrutiny of an officer.

Levi swallowed, and Cheryl watched as his Adam's apple rose and fell. Then he cleared his throat. "But I will tell you. I secured the platform the night before the accident. Someone came behind me and removed those screws."

"Don't worry, Levi. I'll figure out who sabotaged the platform. I'm going to clear your name. And…" Cheryl's voice trailed off. "It'll all work out. I have faith that it will."

Levi placed his calloused hand on the table. More than anything, Cheryl wanted to reach out and wrap her hands around it, but she forced herself to hold back.

"Cheryl, I believe the truth will come out. I cannot imagine what happened. The platform was attached to a frame anchored on two sides—each to a ledger with three joist hangers. They say that all but two of the screws in the joist hangers were removed, so when Rudy stepped up onto the platform, the frame couldn't hold up, and it came down."

"Yes, it happened that quickly," Cheryl said. She tried to picture the platform's construction in her mind.

"Ja, even though I had screwed everything together, the screws were taken out, so the planks had no support under them. Of course they came down as soon as any weight was placed on them. Someone knew what he was doing. He understood how the platform was assembled and knew how to make it appear as if everything was still secure."

"Could they have unscrewed it by hand?"

"There is no way. They would have had to do it with an electric drill, and…" Levi's eyes widened.

"What?"

"I left my drill there, in my toolbox. I hid the toolbox behind the manger next to the gas-powered heater. I was tired and didn't feel like hauling it back and forth to the truck in case there was something I needed to fix in the morning. I thought it would be safe."

"Was it still there yesterday morning?" Cheryl didn't have anything to take notes with, so she tried to remember everything he said.

"When I went back in the morning, I mostly helped with hauling stuff. I brought out the tables that the cookies were on. Oh, and I helped chase sheep. About thirty minutes before everything was to start, I turned on the heater and took my tools back to my truck. I locked them inside, and—"

"And they took your truck for evidence. So I will tell them to check your toolbox for any fingerprints—"

Levi lowered his head. "No, that will do no good."

"What do you mean?"

"Whoever did this knew what they were doing. They knew exactly what to unscrew so that Rudy would fall hard. They had to have planned this. And with the planning, they would have made sure not to leave any fingerprints. This was not just someone playing a prank. It could not have been."

The prisoners at the other tables started standing, and Cheryl knew that their time had ended.

"I know that somehow, somewhere, someone has the answers," she said, trying to encourage Levi.

"More than that, the Good Lord knows the truth," he added.

Hearing Levi say that reminded Cheryl to ask him about hiring a lawyer, but he was quick to shoot down that idea. "My word is the truth, Cheryl. More than that, I have our Lord to defend me. He is a God of justice, remember?"

Cheryl nodded, knowing it would be no use to argue.

"I have been praying that the right person will be caught and punished for their actions. It may be someone we would never expect."

Or someone close to the situation, like Owen Wight, she thought.

They both stood and waited to be escorted out, each in a different direction.

"Levi, I can't believe that I've forgotten to tell you. Yesterday, right before the start of the nativity program, I saw Sarah. She was there with Joe."

"Sarah was there? My sister, Sarah?"

"Yes, and she looked so happy to see us at first. But then things got uncomfortable when Joe came up."

"What do you mean?" He shifted nervously and looked at the police officer walking in their direction.

"Well, I thought Joe would be happy to see us. The few times I've met him before, he's always been kind. I can't remember if he's ever met Rebecca, and I am certain that he's never met Matthew. But he looked at me as if I were a stranger. He didn't even acknowledge the kids. He didn't talk to them at all. He chided Sarah for talking to me about their plans to purchase land in the area. Sarah didn't argue, and then Joe led her to the parking lot…." Cheryl's mind raced. "Where they talked with Owen Wight."

Cheryl didn't have a chance to tell Levi how Sarah and Joe had shown up at their house that afternoon—or at least she thought it was them. The officer came up and motioned for Levi to follow him, and their conversation stopped short.

There was so much she still wanted to say and so much she wanted to ask, yet she couldn't. So instead, Cheryl stood and watched Levi being led away, and part of her heart went with him.

CHAPTER NINE

Cheryl walked out of the police station with slow steps, feeling empty. Leaving her husband at that jail was one of the hardest things she'd ever done. Her body felt weak, as if everything had been drained out of her—all emotion, all energy, all hope. Her stomach growled, reminding her that hunger was part of the problem. She'd had a bowl of cereal for dinner last night, and this morning she'd grabbed an apple on her way out the door. Not much to go on.

She breathed a shallow sigh, imagining what Aunt Mitzi would say if she knew how Cheryl was caring for herself—or, rather, *not* caring for herself. *"You need to eat well and sleep well to think well."* Aunt Mitzi would be right, of course. Cheryl made a mental note to email Aunt Mitzi tonight to tell her what was going on and ask her to pray. How easy it had been to jump into action while forgetting that seeking prayer support from others was just as important.

Cheryl would take care of herself and get lunch. She had thought about opening up the cheese and crackers from Swissters but decided that a sandwich and a hot bowl of soup from the Honey Bee would hit the spot. Out of habit, she parked near the Swiss Miss and walked down the street. It was closer to dinnertime than lunch, but Cheryl knew she'd be better prepared to take care of her kids' needs tonight if she cared for her hunger first.

The clip-clop of horses' hooves blended with the roar of truck engines as Cheryl walked down the sidewalk toward the Honey Bee. The cold wind whipped around her, and she pulled her coat tighter. Her black boots squeaked on the snow as she approached the front door of the quaint café. The aroma of coffee filled the air when she entered. And when she saw who was sitting just two tables from the door, she stopped in her tracks.

Cheryl had never been so excited to see Chief Twitchell sitting at one of the café tables. He was dressed in plain clothes, and he was reading a book while he enjoyed a cup of coffee and worked on a cinnamon roll as large as his head. Cheryl and the chief had become well acquainted over the course of the many mysteries she had helped solve since coming to Sugarcreek. She just wasn't used to seeing him in regular clothes. He looked even taller and lankier than usual, if that was possible.

For a moment, Cheryl considered waiting until the next day to talk to him since Officer Abel had said Chief Twitchell would be back at work then. But something inside told her not to wait. While she'd always felt they had a good relationship as members of the same community, this time, she needed his help as an officer of the law. She needed his help to clear Levi's name.

Cheryl must have been awkwardly standing and staring, because the chief glanced up from his book and lifted his eyebrows. "Cheryl Miller, it seems like something happened when I was off work yesterday, and my guess is that you'd like to talk about it," he said, motioning for her to join him.

That was all the invitation Cheryl needed. She quickly walked over, pulled out the chair opposite him, and sat. "What happened yesterday was awful, just awful. But I know my husband did not do anything to hurt Rudy Wight. I have got to figure this out."

Chief Twitchell tucked a bookmark into the book and then clasped his hands. "Well, Cheryl, you are known around here for putting your nose into other people's business. In a good way, of course. I'm not sure what will happen, but things aren't looking in your husband's favor right now. Levi was the one who built the platform that Rudy stood on. He said he didn't see anyone else tampering with it. But, unfortunately, he was the only one there late the night before the accident, and he arrived early—also before anyone else. That means there was only a small window of opportunity for someone else to tamper with the screws in the platform."

Cheryl gave a hesitant nod but knew better than to interrupt.

"And then, we found used screws in Levi's jacket pocket, the same size as the ones he used for the platform." She opened her mouth to speak to that fact, but Chief Twitchell raised his hand.

Cheryl's body grew rigid. She crossed her legs and forced herself to stay calm. She wouldn't allow herself to argue every little point. She needed the chief for his help and not as a verbal sparring partner.

The chief fiddled with his bookmark, and she could see that he was close to finishing the book. She almost expected him to tell her that they could talk tomorrow, but instead, he shrugged. "Your husband's been doing a lot. He built that whole set. He's runnin' a farm. He's taking care of his wife and children. Even though it might have been an accident, and he simply forgot to screw in the remainin' pieces, it is still negligence. Levi will have to face whatever consequences come from that."

You don't know what you're talking about, she wanted to tell him, but she held her tongue, curled her toes, and nodded. She knew her husband. He did good work. He never did anything haphazardly. Chief Twitchell was right about one thing, though. Levi had been doing a lot.

Still, she didn't believe Levi would ever forget to screw the final pieces to secure a platform. If someone had been intentionally trying to hurt Rudy and place the blame on her husband, she wanted to know why. It was hard to believe how their world had turned upside down and sideways in just two days.

"I understand that Levi will have to face consequences if he is found negligent, but there has to be more that can be done to discover the truth." Cheryl emphasized the last word.

Chief Twitchell closed the cardboard container that held his cinnamon roll and slid it into a to-go bag. He tossed in a plastic fork and a napkin, and then he picked up his book and tucked it under his arm. "I'll tell you what. I'm going back into the office tomorrow, and I'll make it a priority to look over Levi's case first. You make a list of anything you know, and I'll do the same. Then make a list of any questions you have, and I will too. I'll call you sometime in the afternoon, and we'll compare notes. Will that work for you?"

Her eyes bounced from the chief's face to the book, the bag, and back to his face again. She cleared her throat and swallowed the emotion building there. "Yes, of course. I'll look forward to your call."

Cheryl stood and took a step back, letting the chief know she wouldn't bother him with more questions. He rose and moved to the door, but he paused before opening it, turning back to her. "And Cheryl…"

"Yes?" She pushed down the jittery feeling in her stomach.

"It's okay to ask questions and to seek answers. Just be careful." He smiled. "One Miller in trouble with the law is already too much for me."

"Yes, of course, Chief. Thank you."

After Cheryl watched him walk out the door, she got in line to order lunch. She was scanning the menu board when she felt someone walk up behind her. She turned and saw a woman she recognized who often shopped at the Swiss Miss with her mother. "Lori Lynne," Cheryl said, "it's good to see you."

Lori Lynne greeted her with a smile. "Cheryl Cooper. I mean, Cheryl Miller. I'm so glad I ran into you today. Oh my, there's so much going on, and I wanted to check on you to see how you're holding up." The woman's sympathetic gaze bore into Cheryl. The idea that even those who didn't know her well knew what had happened to Levi caused a sense of uneasiness to come over Cheryl. She felt as if she were wearing a sandwich-board sign that read, PATHETIC WOMAN HERE, PLEASE HELP.

Cheryl tried to smile back. "I'm doing as well as can be expected, I guess. You must know about what happened at the church."

"Oh, I heard, and I wanted to get hold of you. Unfortunately, I don't have your cell phone number, and your home phone isn't listed." Lori Lynne fiddled with her beaded necklace that perfectly matched her manicured nails, both a glossy red color.

"Do you have something you want to talk to me about?" Hope surged in Cheryl's heart. "Do you have any information to give me?"

"Yes, actually, I do." Lori Lynne pointed to a table. "Do you have a minute to talk? This is important."

"Of course. Yes, of course." Cheryl moved to the table and sat.

"You might not have heard, but my husband and I divorced last year. I don't know if you knew Tucker—that's my ex-husband's name—but when I was at the nativity opening, it reminded me of so many things. Things I saw. Things I wanted to talk to you about."

Cheryl paused. "So you were there?"

"Yes, and I'm very observant. I saw things I'm certain most people missed. I can make a whole list, but we can save that for another time. Just being there took me back to one of the biggest struggles in my life. And seeing what happened…I knew I had to talk to you."

"Yes, it was just horrible, and to have it happen in front of so many people—"

"I feel terrible for you, Cheryl. And then to see that you had the kids there with you too. It just broke my heart. It took everything in me to stop myself from running to you. I wanted to give you a big hug and tell you everything would be all right. But my mother was with me, and she was having quite a fit. Just being there and seeing everything brought back so many memories for her too."

"So you've faced something like that before?" Cheryl's mind was racing. She couldn't tell if Lori Lynne was talking about the fall or the false accusations against Levi. "Can you tell me about it?"

"Oh, I don't want to go into details. Not here. It's just too gruesome. But I never thought I'd be able to pull myself together again. The pain was so horrible. I felt so broken."

Cheryl leaned closer, finally understanding that Lori Lynne was talking about the fall. Maybe from where she had been standing she had a better view of Rudy. And maybe, because she had faced something similar in her past, she'd noticed something about the platform that others didn't.

Cheryl fixed her gaze on the woman. Pained emotion was evident in the wrinkle of her brows and the downcast of her eyes, but other than that, Lori Lynne was perfectly put together. Cheryl guessed that just went to show how much one could overcome.

"I can tell you were really hurt." Cheryl kept her tone soft. "Yet you got yourself back together. You've made it. Looking at you now, I never would have known."

Lori Lynne tilted her head. "You're not the first to tell me that, but the pain still hits hard sometimes, you know?" She placed her hand over her heart. "And because I know how hard it is, I was hoping you wouldn't mind me talking to you."

"Oh no, of course not. I'd love any information that you have."

"I'm so thankful that you're open to hearing from someone who's been there. Getting what happened out of people's minds is going to be very hard. But know that you will have a support system to help you through."

Cheryl felt warm all over. She'd been so worried that some would get the wrong idea about Levi's involvement in the accident. It was good to know that people still believed in others and didn't judge by appearances. She released a heavy sigh. "I'm so glad you stopped to talk to me. Sometimes I'm so busy thinking about everyone else, especially the kids, that I forget about the help I need too."

"Well, just know that when you're ready, we have a group on Wednesday nights." She leaned in closer as if sharing a secret.

"A group? Wednesday night?" Cheryl's jaw tightened. "But can't you just tell me now? You have the information, and I need it. I'm not sure I can wait."

"I wish it was that easy. I know some people think it's such a black-and-white thing, but the truth is that there are often many people at fault, and our group helps us to accept that."

"I'm not sure what you mean. I'd just assumed there was only one person to blame. Are you telling me that more than one person is involved?"

"There is always more than one person involved." Compassion filled Lori Lynne's eyes. "And that's why the support group is necessary. As hard as it might be, Cheryl, you're partly to blame too. Sadly, lack of communication is always part of it—always. Just know that during the twelve weeks—"

"Twelve weeks?"

"All Divorce Care Groups run in twelve-week cycles. It gives everyone a chance to get on the same page, and—"

"Wait." Cheryl waved both hands, interrupting Lori Lynne. "Did you say 'divorce care'?"

"Yes. I could tell your self-esteem was suffering by what you were wearing in public yesterday, and everyone was a witness to Levi's temper when he argued with Rudy. Then there was the accident, and you ran off instead of going to Levi. I could tell you were afraid of him. And we all know the police have Levi in custody for a reason. I always say that what we see outwardly is just a hint of what's really happening inside the four walls of a home."

"Stop." The word burst from Cheryl's lips. Divorce? She gritted her teeth, trying to remain calm. "So, Lori Lynne, are you telling me that you weren't in an accident—a fall—and that you don't have evidence that will help Levi's case?"

"Me, a fall? No. And I don't have any evidence that would help Levi. Everyone there witnessed what happened." She sighed. "I was talking about recovering from my divorce and overcoming the pain of what I faced in my marriage." Lori Lynne leaned in closer and lowered her voice. "You don't have to pretend anymore that you have a good marriage. Everyone saw the fight between Levi and Rudy. Like I said, we saw Levi's temper—"

"You have no idea what you're talking about." Cheryl stood and raised her voice. "You saw one event, but I know Levi. I know he is innocent and would never purposefully hurt anyone."

The other conversations happening around her stilled, and Cheryl knew that every eye was on her. Yet knowing that didn't bother her as much as realizing that some people believed Levi was guilty—maybe most people.

"I love my husband. I am not getting a divorce. I will never get a divorce." Cheryl peered down her nose at Lori Lynne, expecting her to get upset or angry. Instead, she saw compassion in the woman's gaze, which only made her madder.

Cheryl walked out of the café and stopped on the sidewalk, trying to calm herself. She balled her hands into fists and sucked in a cold breath of air.

The door opened, and Cheryl looked away quickly to hide her tears, but it was too late. Another familiar face met hers. It was Joanna Troyer, Naomi's friend. The two had gone to grade school together and had always been friendly, though they were not incredibly close. Joanna's hair peeked out from under her kapp, and her sweet smile couldn't disguise the curiosity in her eyes as she looked at Cheryl.

It was clear from the look on Joanna's face that she'd overheard what had just happened. Cheryl quickly wiped her cheeks and then pulled on her gloves.

"I'm so sorry. Am I in your way?" Cheryl took a step back so she wouldn't block the door.

"Ne, you are fine, but you do not have any reason to apologize." Joanna spoke with a soft lilt like Naomi, which put Cheryl's heart at ease.

Cheryl pulled her hat down to cover her ears, and then she crossed her arms over her chest. "I should not have caused a scene in there. I should have kept my cool. It just makes me so upset."

"I imagine there is no place you can go that someone doesn't have an opinion about what happened. After all, so many people were there." Joanna reached forward and gently touched Cheryl's elbow. "No one can be prepared for that. There will be more people who just do not understand."

"I'm starting to realize that. I suppose I'm surprised by how some folks are viewing my husband." A sinking feeling in Cheryl's stomach brought dread. Hundreds of people and hundreds of opinions. How could she go anywhere without people talking about her behind their hands? From here on out, would she always question what people thought of Levi?

"I have heard people talking." Joanna's kapp strings fluttered in the cold breeze, and she pulled her collar tighter around her neck. "So far everyone I have talked to has been extremely shocked by what happened."

"And what about you?" Even though it shouldn't have mattered that much, Cheryl desperately wanted to know what Joanna thought. Perhaps even if those in the *Englisch* community had a low opinion of Levi, those in the Amish community would think differently. After all, most of them had known Levi their whole lives. "Surely you know Levi," Cheryl continued. "You know he'd never do anything to hurt another person."

Joanna lifted her chin and clucked her tongue. "I used to know Levi. But, *ach*, he seems a stranger now, driving around in that motorized vehicle and all."

The woman's words hurt nearly as much as a slap across her face, and Cheryl sucked in a breath. But of course, she should have expected this. Levi had left the Amish to marry her, after all. And Sarah had done the same before that.

Cheryl blinked quickly, refusing to let her tears flow. Instead of saying another word, she turned and hurried in the direction of her car. People could believe what they thought, but Cheryl knew the truth. More than that, she would prove the truth.

She hadn't gotten twenty steps before her cell phone rang. She retrieved it from her coat pocket, surprised to see that the call came from her home phone. She quickly answered it.

"Hello?"

"Cheryl, I am so sorry to call." It was Elizabeth. "I think there is something wrong with Rebecca."

"What do you mean? Is she sick? Does she have a fever?"

"No, it is nothing like that. I told her we were going to make a Christmas cake, you know, to celebrate baby Jesus, and when Matthew and I were getting out the ingredients, I turned around and she was gone. I could not find her anywhere, and I have never been so scared." Elizabeth's voice trembled.

"But you found her?"

"Yes, finally. Or at least Judith found her. She came when I went outside and she heard me calling for Rebecca." Elizabeth's voice was still shaking. "Rebecca was hiding in your room—in the closet. She will not come out. She says she does not want to make a birthday cake unless her daed can have a piece too. She wants him to come home and have a piece. Poor *kinder*."

An ache filled Cheryl's chest. "Oh, my sweet girl. It makes sense. We make a Christmas cake every year, and Rebecca always insists that Levi have the first piece."

"Ach, it makes sense why she was so upset then. I am sorry. I did not know."

"Of course you didn't know, and it's not your fault. I should have expected that something like this was going to happen. Rebecca has been trying so hard to believe that things are normal, but I think that, like me, her emotions are finally catching up with her. Can you tell her that I'm coming home and that I'll be there soon?"

"Sure, but don't you have things to do in town today?"

"They can wait. Rebecca needs me home right now. That's where I need to be."

CHAPTER TEN

There were a thousand worries on Cheryl's mind as she prepared to turn down her driveway, and she would have missed the young woman standing on the side of the road next to the white work truck if it hadn't been for the camera in her hands. A professional camera with a zoom lens pointed right at Rudy Wight's property.

Cheryl slowed her vehicle, surprised at first that the young woman didn't turn. The late afternoon sun was lowering on the horizon, but other than that, Cheryl had no idea what she was taking a photo of unless it was the Wight property itself.

She continued her slow turn into the long gravel driveway, now covered with snow, remembering what she'd found on her web search this morning. Rudy Wight's property was worth a pretty penny, far more than Cheryl expected. But was it worth enough that someone would attempt to kill or seriously injure Rudy for it? Maybe someone believed that the property would be easier to obtain from the next of kin with Rudy out of the way. Cheryl knew that people had injured others for far less.

Cheryl continued, driving slowly and watching the young woman from her rearview mirror. Cheryl was about to pass her off as simply a curious tourist when suddenly the young woman turned and started taking photos of the Miller farm too.

Seeing that, Cheryl slammed on the brakes. She hadn't been going very fast, but the sudden movement caused her car to slide to the right. As she considered whether she should drive back and talk to the woman, Cheryl noticed movement in her rearview mirror. She turned in her seat to get a better look and watched as the young woman quickly tucked her camera into its case and then hurried around to the driver's side door. The truck engine started up, and the truck promptly pulled away. As it passed her driveway, Cheryl noticed that some company was advertised on the side of the truck, but from her angle, she had a hard time reading it.

Cheryl frowned and put the car back in drive, reminding herself to tell Levi about this. Once she got inside the house, she needed to make a list of things to discuss with him. But would it matter? She barely had enough time to talk to him about the important stuff. Then again, with all that had been happening lately, it was hard to decide what was important. Maybe the young woman did have something to do with Rudy's accident.

She considered something Lori Lynne had said—the one good point she made before Cheryl realized that the woman had been trying to invite her to a divorce-care group instead of providing her with information that could help Levi. Lori Lynne had sparked the idea that more than one person could be involved. Did that include this photographer woman too?

Cheryl gripped the steering wheel as faces flashed through her mind. Owen, Joe, and now this young woman. One of them could be involved, or all of them. Cheryl had a hard time believing Sarah was involved, and she would have doubted Joe's involvement too if it hadn't been for the strange way he'd acted when he saw her. At this point, Cheryl had to keep her mind open to all possibilities. The only possibility she wasn't open to was that Levi was guilty after all. She couldn't allow herself to go there or imagine what it would mean if she somehow couldn't prove his innocence.

Elizabeth was in the kitchen with Matthew when Cheryl entered.

"Mama, birdies! Wook!" He waved peanut-butter-covered hands and smiled. More peanut butter was smeared on his face.

"Oh, that looks like fun." She attempted to keep her tone light and focus on her son instead of the questions she had about the young woman who'd been taking photos.

Elizabeth and Matthew were making birdseed hangers. They used cookie cutters to cut shapes out of bread, covered the shapes with peanut butter, then rolled them in birdseed. When finished, they'd hang them on the porches for the winter birds. Watching the birds was one of Matthew's favorite things to do.

It made her heart happy to know at least one member of their family was enjoying life and having fun. If only she could live in the moment, even for a short time. She released a sigh at the thought.

Cheryl stepped into the kitchen, kissed Matthew on the forehead, and then immediately hurried to her bedroom. Sure enough, Rebecca was in the closet, curled in a ball with her back pressed against the corner.

Cheryl removed her hat and coat. Then she lowered herself to the ground, sat cross-legged, and opened her arms.

Rebecca's eyes fixed on Cheryl, but she didn't budge. Instead, she shook her head and crossed her arms. She sniffled, wiped her nose with her sleeve, and then looked away.

"Boo, it'll be all right. Daddy will be home soon." Cheryl forced a smile, which she hoped Rebecca believed. The truth was, she wanted to climb in there with her and hide away. Withdrawing seemed much easier than trying to figure everything out.

"But I heard you talking to Oma. You said you were worried about Christmas. You said things could go wrong. You said Daddy might not come home."

Cheryl reached out and stroked her daughter's hair back from her face. "I know, but I shouldn't have said that. I need to have faith. We both need to have faith."

"Auntie Elizabeth tried to be happy, but her eyes were sad too." Rebecca uncrossed her arms. "We don't have a tree, and I wanna put up pretty Christmas things. Auntie Elizabeth said we couldn't play in the snow because you would get sad if we got sick. And for three days I've wanted to make Christmas cookies."

"Three days, huh?" Cheryl tried not to smile. "I thought you didn't like making all those cookies, pressing them out with the cookie cutters. You said it was too much work."

"But I like to decorate them," Rebecca said, scooting closer. "I like sprinkles."

"I know you do, and I'll tell you what. I might need to go to town again tomorrow, to help Daddy, but I will make sure that I bake or find some cookies for us to decorate. Is that a deal?"

Instead of answering, Rebecca crawled out of the closet, over Levi's dress shoes, and climbed into Cheryl's lap, tucking her head under Cheryl's chin. "But can we wait to make the Christmas cake? You know Daddy always has to have the first piece."

Cheryl wound a finger around one of her daughter's curls. "Of course we can wait, and you can ask Daddy what kind of cake he wants this year. Chocolate or vanilla, it's always hard to choose."

Rebecca lifted her face to meet Cheryl's gaze with a smile on her face, yet it pained Cheryl to see it. She released the curl and pulled Rebecca closer, tighter, wishing to protect her from any heartache or pain.

She had made the promise of somehow getting cookies tomorrow, and she would figure that out. She just hoped that she hadn't hurt things more than helped when she told her daughter that they would be able to bake a cake for Levi this year. It was easy to make promises to Rebecca. Harder would be keeping them. Then again, if Levi was charged, a judge might consider letting him out on bond for Christmas, unless Levi refused. Her husband, like all Amish, didn't believe in going into debt with anyone.

Finally, after some coaxing, Cheryl convinced Rebecca to help Matthew finish the birdseed cutouts. When they made their way back into the kitchen, Matthew was still playing in the birdseed. Elizabeth had moved to the stove, and she hummed an Amish hymn as she served up steamy bowls of navy bean soup. Cheryl's stomach growled, and she sat down at the table where Elizabeth had placed a bowl for her. Finally, after a busy day, she was getting something to eat.

"This looks wonderful, Elizabeth. You're a godsend."

"I am glad to help. It is the least I can do. Although I will say the kids will be happy to have you here." She set a bowl of soup down for Rebecca and then leaned closer. "See, didn't I tell you your mama would come home right away if I called her?"

Rebecca picked up her spoon and then put it down again, hanging her head. "Yeah, but not Daddy."

"Not your daddy, at least not yet." Elizabeth kept her tone light. "Any news, Cheryl?" Elizabeth sat down with her soup and a bowl of crackers she placed between them.

Cheryl nodded. "Rebecca, Matthew, I saw your daddy, and he told me to give you both big hugs. And…" She scrambled for what to say next. What could she say to give them hope? Thankfully, the sound of footsteps on the front porch caught everyone's attention. Even Matthew stopped playing with the birdseed and turned to the front door.

Naomi bustled into the room and Seth followed, his cheeks pink and eyes bright. Naomi wore a gray cloak over her dress, a dark brown scarf, dark brown mittens, and a black bonnet over her kapp. She looked plain in every way, but the joy and peace on her face brightened the room. Seeing Naomi's smile warmed Cheryl's heart just as the soup warmed her body.

"We have come to pick up Elizabeth, but oh my, something smells good."

"Maam, there's soup," Elizabeth said. "Warm yourself up before we head out again."

Naomi removed her mittens, scarf, and bonnet. She unbuttoned her cloak and hung it on the coatrack. Seth excused himself to do the afternoon chores, saying he'd be back shortly. Emotion pinched Cheryl's heart with gratefulness for Levi's family and the way they cared for her.

"I could have driven Elizabeth home," Cheryl said. "I wouldn't have minded. But then again, I'm thankful for the company and for Seth doing the chores. I'd have no idea where to start."

Instead of moving to the stove to ladle soup, Naomi hurried to the table to give Cheryl's shoulder a warm squeeze. But, even though she didn't mean to, Cheryl stiffened at her friend's touch.

"My dear, you feel as if you are a ball of tense nerves."

Cheryl reached and squeezed the back of her neck, for the first time realizing how sore it was. Naomi was right. Her whole body felt tight with tension.

She reached across the table to a notebook and pen that had been there since she'd made a grocery list a week ago. "I think it's because I have all these questions and worries wound up in my head. I need to write everything down to keep track. There have to be some answers, or at least one answer somewhere."

"That is a good idea. You write, and I'll eat, and then we can talk about what you have there."

Cheryl wrote down a list, all questions.

Argument at church, property line?
Who would want to hurt Rudy?
Levi targeted for blame. Why?
Why did the sale of the Wight property fall through?
Who would benefit from the sale? Realtor? Family? Other?

Desperate purchaser?
Owen Wight involved?

Cheryl paused, and she thought about writing down Sarah's and Joe's names but decided not to, knowing Naomi would read what she wrote. Cheryl didn't want to tell Naomi about seeing them. Or about their visit to the farm either. She wanted to reach out to Sarah and talk to her first. So next to Owen's name she simply wrote *Others?* And then she continued.

Security cameras?
Levi's truck taken for evidence?
Missing screws? Fingerprints on Levi's toolbox?
No eyewitnesses?

And then Cheryl decided to add a few more things. She didn't know if they were connected, yet they still bothered her.

Man watching me at the Swiss Miss?
Young woman taking photos?
Amish community upset with Levi leaving the church?

Naomi glanced with curiosity at the paper as Cheryl wrote, and Cheryl handed it her direction when she was done. Naomi's fingertips fluttered to her lips as she read. "It seems there are many questions but no answers."

Cheryl nibbled at the corner of her lip. "That's all I have—questions."

"So signs are still pointing to Levi?"

"If I didn't know him well…" Cheryl allowed her voice to trail off, and then she noticed Rebecca's gaze intent on her. "I'm sure there are answers. I just need time to think and to figure it out. I—"

Rebecca sat with her spoon in her hand, but she didn't take a bite. As Cheryl glanced around, she noticed that both Elizabeth and even Matthew were watching her, waiting to hear what else she was about to say. Cheryl opened her mouth, but no words emerged.

Seeing her distress, Naomi stood from her seat with a flourish. "Oh, I almost forgot. I was going to invite you children over tomorrow, but now that I am thinking about it, I could use some help tonight." She looked from Rebecca to Matthew and back to Rebecca again. "Our barn cat had kittens a few weeks ago, and Opa said the temperature is dropping low tonight. I think we should bring them in. I was not sure how I was to care for six kittens tonight, and I was wondering if you two would be helpers. What do you think about coming to stay the night?"

Cheryl watched as her children's eyes grew wide with excitement.

At the same time, surprise registered on Elizabeth's face. "Daed is letting us bring the kittens in the house?" Her eyes widened as she glanced at her niece. "Rebecca, this is a first."

Naomi cast a tight smile at Elizabeth as if urging her to play along. "It is a good idea, don't you think? The kittens are starting to crawl around. And their eyes are open. I would sure like some helpers to assist me in keeping them out of trouble. Is anyone here interested?"

"Me!" both of Cheryl's children called, and, as if sensing the excitement, Beau emerged from Rebecca's room where he'd been napping. He padded over to Naomi and rubbed against her stockinged legs with a meow. Giggles emerged from the children at the sight.

Rebecca scooped him up and squeezed him. "Not you, Beau."

"No, no, Beau!" Matthew added, jumping up and down and scattering birdseed as he did.

Naomi turned to her. "Is that okay with you, Cheryl, if the children come as my helpers? I am sorry, I know I should have asked you first."

Cheryl waved her hand in Naomi's direction. "Yes, it's fine. I'll miss them, but it sounds like fun." Then, as the children ran to their room to get their pajamas, Cheryl said, "Thank you."

Naomi brushed her thanks aside. "We will make a plan tomorrow to talk over your list, but for tonight do your best to get some rest. Take some time and pray, asking the Lord to direct your thoughts. And remember, you are not in this alone. There are so many people who love Levi and you both. Seth and I will continue to help until Levi is home, which I hope will be sooner than we all expect."

"Thank you, Naomi." Cheryl put her pen down. "It's only been two days, but it seems like it's been twenty. Let's also remember to pray for Rudy Wight and his family too. After all, he's the one who was hurt. I just wish I knew more about how he's doing."

Naomi paused, turning back. "Oh, I did hear from my friend Betty. Her husband is at the hospital recovering from surgery, and she said that Rudy is still in intensive care. Betty talked to Rudy's wife. Do you know her? I heard she is a very nice lady. But Betty said that she did not know if Rudy had come out of his coma or not. Things are still touch-and-go."

"Isn't Betty a scribe for *The Budget*?" Cheryl asked.

"Yes, one from our area."

"So that means we'll all be able to get more details when it's published."

Naomi nodded, and when a crashing noise came from Matthew's bedroom, she hurried in that direction. Even amid a crisis, there were always a couple of things Cheryl could count on. Matthew making messes, and getting all the latest news from *The Budget*, a newspaper for the Amish and Mennonites, even when she couldn't get information from anywhere else.

Less than an hour after Seth and Naomi had arrived, they left with Elizabeth, Rebecca, and Matthew. Naomi and Elizabeth had made sure they'd left behind a clean kitchen too.

Cheryl sank into her chair, wondering what she should focus on first. There was so much to think about, to worry about. She knew she needed prayer most. She pulled out her phone and sent a short text to her parents. She didn't want to go into too many details with them. She didn't have the energy to talk to her mom on the phone for an hour, answering her questions. Cheryl also knew she needed to ask Aunt Mitzi to pray too. Although Aunt Mitzi preferred letters, Cheryl didn't have time for that.

Instead, she opened a new email on her phone. *Dear Aunt Mitzi, please, please, would you pray?* And then, typing out the message with her thumbs, she poured out her worries.

After Cheryl hit send, the words of a hymn floated through her thoughts.

> *We've a little song for Jesus, pray will you hear?*
> *If you'll listen we will sing it, loudly and clear.*
> *Jesus loves us, our dearest friend!*
> *'Tis on Him that our hopes depend.*

She tried to remember when she'd first heard it. Oh yes, it had been one of the songs sung by the visiting choir from Papua New Guinea. It seemed like decades ago when she'd sat by Levi's side, listening. Her hand had rested in his, and at that moment, she had felt content. She had trusted back then that Jesus heard her prayers. Yet had God changed? No, He was still there, still the same, and the song flowing through her heart reminded her that He desired to be her dearest friend, no matter what happened.

"'Tis on Him that our hopes depend," Cheryl whispered into the quiet room around her. Yes, she had her list to hold, but she needed to remember that it was God holding her. For a moment, Cheryl thought about going over her list once more, but instead, she chose to be content. She allowed her heart to fill with thankfulness for her Lord, her family, and her husband, whether she had all the answers or not.

CHAPTER ELEVEN

Outside the window the following day, the world was silent beneath a blanket of snow. Peaks of white covered the farmhouses and barns like frosting. One lone trail, made from boot prints, ran from the parking area—where Judith's car was parked—to the dawdy haus. A pang of guilt pierced Cheryl's heart. How many days had it been since she'd talked to Judith face-to-face? Too many. Her friend had come for a month to truly enjoy the Christmas season. Cheryl just hoped that she didn't regret coming.

Even before the accident, Cheryl had been so busy trying to keep up with the kids while Levi had been out of the house. And then his arrest changed everything. Her mind was so busy trying to figure out what had happened that she hadn't even thought about checking on her friend.

Cheryl threw on her jacket, pulled her hat onto her head, and quickly stepped into her boots. She hurried outside and then rushed over to the dawdy haus. She knocked on the door, but even before it opened, wonderful smells drifted out.

The door swung wide, and Judith greeted her with a smile, waving her in. "Oh good, you're here. I have so many trays for you."

Cheryl stepped in and shut the door behind her. She started to ask what Judith meant, but scanning the kitchen and small dining table made the question unnecessary. Trays of Christmas treats—sugar cookies, fudge, peanut brittle, and more—covered every flat surface.

Cheryl laughed. "What is all this?"

"I love to bake. It's one of my favorite things to do. A few days ago, Levi asked if he could pick up anything from the store for me. I told him flour, sugar, and a few other items for baking. He must be used to shopping for you or his mother, because he came home with twenty pounds of flour and more sugar than I could use in a month of Sundays. I considered telling him to take most of it to your place, but then I felt a nudge to use it."

Cheryl took in another deep breath of all the wonderful smells as she listened. Her heart warmed, thinking of how kind Levi had been to Judith. *It's just like him.*

"I remember what it was like to be a young mom," Judith continued. "I'd burn almost every cookie to a crisp, mostly because I was so busy chasing kids that I'd forget I had put something in the oven." She smiled. "But all that to say, I guessed that your children would like some sugar cookies to decorate. And I made some of my other favorite recipes too." Judith picked up a piece of fudge. "This is my grandmother's recipe. Christmas isn't Christmas without it."

Cheryl gave Judith a hug. "Oh, Judith. Just last night Rebecca asked if we could decorate cookies. I told her that we would sometime, but I had no idea how God would provide." She placed a hand over her heart. "Thank you. I didn't know that Levi went to the store for you. That's just something he—" Emotion caught in Cheryl's throat. "That's just something Levi would do."

"Levi is all right, isn't he? Was he able to help those officers? I haven't seen his truck in a couple of days."

"There was an accident at the nativity." Cheryl attempted to explain the whole thing. Her friend listened intently, and when Cheryl was done explaining what happened, Judith offered to pray. Cheryl gave Judith a big hug and then looked around. "Can I pick these up later? I really need to run. There are some things I need to check into, for Levi."

"Don't worry about that, Cheryl. Just leave your door unlocked. I'll take them all over."

"Are you sure?"

"Yes, I'm sure. I'm retired, remember? I have all day. You just do what you have to do and don't worry about a thing."

Cheryl hurried back to her house, and she did what Judith asked. She walked away from her home and didn't look back. Today she wouldn't think about Christmas and all the things that needed to get done. Instead, she had ideas of people to talk to who might have insight into what happened between Rudy and Levi. She had a feeling that understanding more about their conflict would help her know where to look next. She had questions about the Wight property too.

But before she started her car, Cheryl searched for Sarah's contact info on her phone and tapped the number. The phone rang four times, and then it went to voice mail. "Hello, this is Sarah. Sorry to miss you. You know what to do."

Sarah's voice seemed so light and happy in her recorded message. But she'd seemed the exact opposite when Cheryl saw her at the nativity set. For so many years, Cheryl had imagined that no news was good news from Sarah. But now she wondered if that was true.

The phone beeped, and Cheryl cleared her throat. "Hi Sarah, this is Cheryl. It was so good to talk to you the other day. It was such a fun surprise, and I was calling..." She paused for a moment, deciding what step she wanted to take. "I was calling to see if you would like to stop by the house sometime. I'd love to talk with you, and the kids would love to see you. Let me know if you're available anytime soon. Call me back."

She ended the call and then placed the phone in her coat pocket. Just knowing she had taken one small step made her feel a bit better. Of course, if Sarah didn't respond right away, Cheryl would need to consider the next move she should make. But for now, the ball was in Sarah's court.

This morning, Cheryl had prioritized heading to Sugarcreek Realty first. While there were a lot of small questions, she needed to understand the bigger picture. She knew that the Wight property had been for sale, but it had been taken off the market for some reason. Had it sold already? If not, would someone want that property so badly that they'd be willing to hurt the owner? If so, why? And what, if anything, did the Realtor know?

CHAPTER TWELVE

Cheryl pulled her scarf down and cast a quick smile at the man who sat at the large desk at Sugarcreek Realty. His phone was pressed to his ear, and his eyebrows were furrowed.

"Just a minute. I'll be right there," he called to her. His voice sounded friendly enough.

With the phone pressed to his ear, the man rose and moved to a back room.

Cheryl looked around, noting that the space was sparse. Two chairs sat in front of the desk, and a drab couch and end table had been positioned near the front window. She settled onto the couch, perched on the front of the cushion, picturing how much she could brighten up the place with some items from the Swiss Miss.

Just adding a lap quilt over the back of the couch and throw pillows would be a nice touch. She also had carved walnut candle-sticks that would look perfect on the end table. And of course some Christmas decorations around the room would do wonders. Cheryl couldn't imagine not taking the effort to buy a wreath for the door, especially since every other business in Sugarcreek deco-rated for Christmas with gusto.

She glanced at the wall across from her, imagining how ador-able it would look if the plain bulletin board was framed with wood to look like a window. Then the photos of properties could be cleverly displayed. But, unfortunately, the six pictures of houses and one piece of property looked like they'd been haphazardly posted on the corkboard.

Just as she'd straightened the pictures in her mind, the man walked back into the main room. The frown he'd been wearing earlier was gone. A huge smile was plastered to his face instead. "Hello. Chilly day out there, isn't it? I'm Rich Chetty. How can I help you?"

"I'm here to talk to you about a piece of property in Sugarcreek."

"You are? Okay, well, they're all up there." Rich pointed to the corkboard. "Very few things are for sale right now in Sugarcreek." His lips tilted down. "But there are a few nice houses in the surrounding area if you're interested in those."

"Oh, the property I wanted to ask about isn't up there. However, I believe it was available a few months ago—a beautiful piece of land over on Miller Road."

"That… Yes, well, you're right that it's not available." His frown returned full force. "I'm sorry, but it would be better if we didn't discuss that. Losing that deal ruined everything, especially my Christmas."

"So you're saying that it was listed but it fell through?"

"Fell through?" He spoke through clenched lips. "I was robbed. Robbed of a sale. A big developer was going to give us top dollar. I was robbed of giving my kids the Christmas I promised them and my wife the trip to see her parents in Florida." He pressed his fingertips to his forehead. "Do you have any idea how frustrating it is to have your business practically ruined because of one person?"

Frustrating enough to hurt someone? The words flew through Cheryl's mind. "Surely these things happen sometimes." She kept her voice gentle, trying to soothe the man.

"It was the neighbor's fault."

Cheryl's chest tightened. "And why would you say that?" She slipped her hands into her coat pockets, hoping to hide their shaking. *Could this be it?*

"I can't give any details. But one man's thoughtless actions turned a beautiful piece of property into an eyesore."

Cheryl tilted up her chin. "Surely the neighbor tried to negotiate a solution first."

"Whether he did or didn't isn't my concern. My kids, my wife, and now this dreadful Christmas," Rich spat. "He'll pay though. What goes around, comes around."

"What do you mean, he'll pay?" Emotion caused her voice to raise an octave.

Rich looked at Cheryl. "Who are you again?"

"I'm someone who wanted to ask you questions about a piece of property. But I think I need to go somewhere else. You don't seem to be able to help me."

The man's jaw fell slack. "Well, wait. You really are interested in something? I thought you were someone from the Chamber of Commerce. They've been harassing me to decorate this place. Do they think I'm made of money? Why would I spend money putting up a fake tree in my office when I have nothing for my kids' stockings?" Rich's face fell, and suddenly her heart filled with compassion for him.

"It seems this hasn't been an easy year for you. It must be hard when you believe that someone ruined a big sale. Do you think..." She paused, trying to figure out how to phrase her question. "Well, since the owner of the property was in a serious accident, do you think his wife or his son will put it back on the market? And that the sale may be able to go through after all?"

"What do you mean, accident?" Rich looked at her, confused. "Are you talking about Mr. Wight? I haven't heard anything about an accident."

"Yes, he was in an accident two days ago, down at Community Bible Church. I've heard from others that he's still in critical condition."

"No, that's impossible." The words shot from the man's mouth. He sat hard on one of the chairs. "I just saw him last night."

Cheryl's mouth dropped open. "You saw him last night?"

"I stopped to get gas last night, and he was exiting the gas station. I'd recognize him anywhere."

Cheryl sat back on the sofa. "You couldn't have seen Rudy Wight. What did the man at the gas station look like?"

"He had light brown hair and wire-rimmed glasses." He frowned at her.

The face of the man who'd been in the Swiss Miss filled Cheryl's mind. "We can't be talking about the same man. The Mr. Wight I know doesn't wear wire-rimmed glasses or have light brown hair. He's older with no glasses and gray hair. Well, what hair he still has is gray."

Rich pointed a finger at her. "Listen, I don't know who you are or what you're here for. It seems like you're up to something else and not looking to buy property at all. Why are you asking so many questions?"

"I never said I was looking to *buy* property. I said I was interested in a piece of property—in information about it. But I think you've given me the information I need." Cheryl rose, and Rich did the same. He rushed to the door, and for a moment, she thought he was going to block her exit, but thankfully, he opened the door for her and waved her through.

As soon as Cheryl exited, she heard the click of the door locking behind her. Then the lights in Sugarcreek Realty dimmed. Even though it wasn't quite noon, Rich Chetty was shutting down for the day. Had something she said spooked him or caused him to run? What she did know was that someone out there was trying to pass himself off as Rudy Wight, and she had a feeling that one of her next steps needed to be figuring out who and why.

CHAPTER THIRTEEN

Cheryl hurried, weaving through Christmas shoppers whose arms were laden with goods. She hadn't done much shopping herself, and she honestly didn't know when that would be possible. How could she even think about picking out baby dolls and toy dump trucks when her husband sat in jail?

She hadn't gotten more than twenty steps away from the realty office when her phone rang. Her mind still raced with the knowledge that someone pretending to be their neighbor had been the one negotiating with the Realtor concerning the Wights' property. Who would do that? And why? Did Rudy know? Did Owen? She pushed all those questions out of her mind to answer the phone.

"Hello?" Her voice rose as she answered, and her feet quickened their pace. *More questions. Why more questions?* She needed more answers.

"Cheryl?"

She recognized the chief's voice immediately and stopped walking. "Yes, Chief Twitchell?"

He'd said he'd call her this afternoon. Was something wrong? Was that why he was calling early?

"Is everything all right, Chief?" she hurriedly asked.

"You sound like you're winded, Cheryl. I should ask you the same."

"Oh, I'm just going around town trying to figure things out." Cheryl didn't tell him about what she'd just discovered at Sugarcreek Realty. She still needed time to process it herself.

"It's good that you're already in town. I came in really early this morning, so I've had a chance to sort things out. Do you have time to talk?"

"I'm not far from the Honey Bee Café. Would it be possible to meet and talk there? I'm starving." Again, she'd forgotten to eat, to take care of herself as she should.

"Actually, I have some things to show you over here at the police station. So why don't you get some lunch for yourself and meet me here? Just tell Kathy to put it on my tab. And if you don't mind, can you also bring one of those cinnamon rolls?"

"I thought officers were supposed to like donuts best." She chuckled at her joke, resuming her pace.

"That may be true for those who haven't tasted Kathy's cinnamon rolls. See you soon."

Thirty minutes later, Cheryl was sitting in Chief Twitchell's office. She enjoyed a cup of chicken noodle soup while he dug into his cinnamon roll.

"So, Cheryl, I've heard that you've been going around asking businesses if they caught anything on their security cameras. More than one business owner called and asked me if it was all right to give you the information, but I told them to just go ahead and bring it down to the station instead."

Cheryl looked his way sheepishly. "Yes, well, they are my friends. I thought they might be able to help." She took another sip from her spoon.

"I've told you before, that's our job. We are going to complete our investigation, and I hope we do find something that will prove Levi's innocence. But right now, you just have to let us do our job."

"So if you found out I was asking around about security cameras, does that mean those business owners found something?" She set her cup of soup down and scooted to the edge of her chair. "Did you find anything, you know, official?"

"Yes, we found something, and I have to say it doesn't look good for Levi." He took another bite of his cinnamon roll as if he hadn't just dropped a bombshell.

Cheryl sucked in a breath and pushed her soup away, no longer hungry. "What do you mean?"

"We found out that someone was there between the time that Levi said he left and when he returned. We couldn't see what the person was doing, but they approached the back of the nativity set where the platform had been set up."

Cheryl dared to ask. "Can you tell who it is? Can I look at it?"

"Yes, I will show you in a few minutes. And I want you to know that we've already shown the video to Levi. He says that he was home sleeping, and said you will tell the same story."

"Yes, he was home sleeping," she answered without hesitation.

Chief Twitchell set his fork down and pushed the cinnamon roll to the side. "And can you remember when he came in?"

She squirmed in her seat. "What do you mean? Like, exactly what time?" She tilted her head.

"Do you know what time Levi came home the night before the accident, Cheryl?" Chief Twitchell leaned forward with his elbows on his desk. "It's not that hard a question."

"I remember him coming in, and, uh… I remember he was cold from being outside. He snuggled under the covers, and…" She searched her mind for something more, but there was nothing. She was pretty sure she hadn't even opened her eyes. "I can't really say…."

The chief rested his chin on his fists. "Do you even have a general idea what time your husband got in?"

Cheryl had a decision to make. Should she make up a number? Hadn't Levi said he'd been home around eleven thirty? She could just say that.

Yet she thought about what Levi would want her to do. He would want her to tell the truth. "Actually, I don't know. I didn't wake up enough to look at the clock. I don't remember because I was sleeping. I stirred, but I didn't look at the clock," she repeated.

The chief nodded, and then he leaned back in his chair, placing his hands on his lap. "Yes, Levi said the same thing. He said you wouldn't be able to give him an alibi for the time." Without saying anything else, the sheriff typed something into his computer, turned the monitor so Cheryl could see, and pressed play. There was a black-and-white image, and a view of the nativity set was apparent. White flakes of snow softly drifted downward. Then motion, as the long strides of a man walked toward the nativity set. He paused by the manger, although Cheryl couldn't see what he was doing, and then he walked around to the back, out of the camera's view.

After a few minutes, the man returned to the front by the manger. It looked as if he'd set something there. Then he left again, walking toward the parking lot—the way he had come.

It was evident that the man was tall and broad-shouldered—just like Levi—but the image was too blurry to see who it was. The jacket seemed to be similar to the one that Levi wore too. Immediately, Cheryl knew it wasn't Owen, who was shorter and much wirier than the man on the screen.

The chief paused the video. Cheryl's shoulders slumped, and she looked down at her lap. "I guess you can't rule out Levi. Although you really can't tell who it is by looking at this video. It's clear to see it's not Owen."

"Owen Wight, Rudy's son? Why do you think it would be him?"

Cheryl explained the odd way Owen had acted right after the accident, and Chief Twitchell listened with interest. She even saw him jot down a few notes. However, she didn't mention Joe and Sarah, even though they had met up with Owen at the event. Cheryl was still waiting to talk to Sarah. She wanted to hear the explanation in Sarah's own words about what was going on. It was the least she could do for family.

"We can be sure that Owen Wight wasn't the one who did something to the platform, but we can't rule out his involvement. I agree that his actions were very odd."

"And what about other cameras? Are there any others in the area that we can look at?" she asked.

"There are others, but none of them have a good view. This is the clearest view we have. I'm sorry. I wish I had better news."

"And I wish I would have paid attention to the time when Levi arrived home and left again. It's funny how things you never thought would matter make a big difference later." She folded her hands on the desk.

"I appreciate that you're trying to help, Cheryl, but you need to know we're doing our job. I'm sorry to tell you this, but the case was brought before the district attorney. There is enough evidence for us to officially press charges against Levi."

"What does that mean?"

"The law is that we can only hold someone for seventy-two hours without pressing charges. We would have had to let Levi go today—"

"What about bail?" Cheryl asked.

The chief looked uncomfortable. "In a case like this, when we're talking about attempted harm or even murder—"

"Murder!" Cheryl was horrified to hear the word spoken out loud in relation to Levi.

"The man is in critical condition, Cheryl," the chief said gently. "He could have easily been killed, and we have to assume, until we know differently, that that's what was intended. The bail, unfortunately, is set pretty high in a case like this, and even payin' just the 10 percent to get Levi home is prohibitive. I've already discussed it with Levi, and he refuses to go into any kind of debt to get himself out of jail."

"So he's staying…"

"Until a trial."

"Or until he's proven innocent?"

"Yes, there's always that." Chief Twitchell sighed. "But if we didn't think there was still a lot of evidence pointin' to Levi, he would be out of here. Also, he told me he didn't want to hire an attorney. He said it was no use paying someone to provide the truth in defense when he could do that himself."

Cheryl froze, a sinking feeling coming over her. *Oh, Levi.*

"But then I told him about the public defender who is provided free of charge. I explained to Levi that their job is more than just telling the truth."

"And…" She held her breath.

"Levi agreed to talk to the public defender, although the soonest we can make that happen is after Christmas."

She nodded, wishing she could hold Levi's hand and that they could go through this side by side. *Hopefully I'll find the proof to get him out before it comes to that.*

She refused to cry and took another deep breath instead. Then, gaining her composure, she looked at the chief. "Yesterday when I left, the officer couldn't tell me exactly when I'd be able to see Levi again. Do you happen to know when?"

The chief stood. "Sooner than you think. They just finished questioning him, and I told Officer Abel that I thought you'd want to see him."

Cheryl jumped to her feet. "Thank you. After the disappoint-ment with the video, that's a bit of good news." She moved toward the door, but the chief held up his hand.

"There are some things you should know." He folded his arms over his chest. "After watching the video, Levi admitted he'd left his toolbox behind the manger in the nativity."

"Yes, he told me that too. So, on the video, that's what he—whoever that person is—was getting when he first got there—the toolbox?" It made sense.

"Yes, and then the person returned it. Levi also told us he'd put the toolbox in his truck about an hour before the event was due to start. So it was in his truck when we brought it in."

Cheryl fixed her eyes on the chief's, wondering what this was leading up to.

"Inside the toolbox, we found the screws that had been in the joist. They were inch-and-a-half screws, just what Levi claims he used."

"So the screws in his jacket pocket…"

"They weren't the right ones. But the fact that the screws were in his truck is more evidence against him."

"But isn't it obvious? Whoever took out the screws put them in Levi's toolbox to frame him."

"But the only fingerprints we could find were Levi's."

"So what you're telling me is that the person had been watch-ing Levi. They knew where he'd put his tools. And they were very careful not to leave fingerprints."

"Which could be possible, but in my experience, the right solution is usually the most simple one. Levi had a motive, he had means, and he had the opportunity. I just wanted to let you know how things stood before I take you back to see him. As you can guess, he's feeling pretty dejected. I was hoping you could cheer him up."

"And do you believe he did it, Chief Twitchell?"

"Cheryl, my job is not based on what I believe. It's based on what the evidence says."

A few minutes later, she was sitting in the same room she had been in with Levi just the day before. She told him about the help she'd gotten from Elizabeth, Judith, and his parents. She also told him about how Rebecca had hidden in his closet when Elizabeth had tried to bake a Christmas cake with her, which brought a tear to his eye.

"Oh my goodness, I can't believe that I almost forgot to tell you this again."

"What?" Levi stroked the stubble on his chin, looking extremely tired.

Cheryl told Levi about seeing Sarah and Joe at the event. "I still think it's very odd the way Owen Wight acted. He seemed more concerned about getting you in trouble than about even checking to see if his father was all right. And when Sarah and Joe went to the parking lot, they were talking to Owen. Isn't that strange? The man in the video footage was too large to be Owen, but he was around Joe's size."

Levi lifted his hands. "Wait a minute. What are you saying? Do you really believe that my brother-in-law could have done something like this?"

"I do know that you didn't do it, so I'm willing to entertain any thought of who could have done it instead."

"Yes, Cheryl, but Joe is in law enforcement. I think the last time I talked to him he was a detective, or something like that."

"And who better than a detective would know how to commit the perfect crime?"

Levi rubbed his bloodshot eyes. "You must not be getting enough sleep. You are not making any sense."

"But why would Joe be talking to Owen? Maybe they met when Joe was out looking at property. Maybe they thought if they could get Rudy out of the way, they could develop a plan that would benefit them both."

"Still, Joe doesn't seem like the kind of person who would do something like that."

"Yes, but maybe they just wanted to hurt him a little, just to make him lame enough that he wouldn't be able to take care of his property."

Levi stroked his chin again. "Well, that might make a little sense. It also makes sense why Owen would run to the police. If he genuinely did not think his father would be injured very badly, then I suppose his biggest worry would be to make sure that I looked guilty instead of them."

Cheryl nodded, but as she did, she understood that proving such a thing would be very difficult. After all, it was Levi and Rudy who had been in an argument right before the accident happened. She also considered telling Levi that Joe and Sarah had gone to their house when they weren't there, but she decided to wait. She didn't want him to have too many objections about what she wanted to tell him next.

"I already tried to reach out to Sarah. I left a message on her phone, but she hasn't called me back."

Levi's eyes widened. "You don't think she has anything to do with this, do you?"

"No, I really don't. And honestly, I'm hoping that this theory isn't true either. As much as I'd like to make sure you're home for Christmas, I don't want to think that another family member is responsible. There's enough strain in the relationship with Sarah and your parents as it is."

"Then what are you going to say to her?"

"Actually, I'm going to see if she would like to come over or meet up with me and the kids. Now that she lives close, there's no reason why Rebecca and Matthew shouldn't know their aunt Sarah."

"Do you think she will meet with you?"

"I have a hunch that if she can do it without letting Joe know, she will. But I have another reason to see her. Aunt Mitzi included them in the presents she sent us this year. Out of all the people to send extra gifts to, would you believe that she included ones for Sarah and Joe?"

"That seems somewhat out of the ordinary, but it also seems like something your aunt Mitzi would do. She always seems more in touch with God than most, as if they have some secret plans that only later the two of them let others in on."

"Yes, and hopefully whatever Sarah tells me will rule out any notions that we have about them being involved in Rudy's accident."

"*We* have?" Levi chuckled. "I thought these were all the things *you* are investigating."

"That's true, but we're a team, aren't we?"

Levi leaned close as if he wanted to kiss her, and then he paused. She wasn't sure if anyone was on the other side of the glass watching, and even though Levi was apparently fine discussing possible suspects and their motives, he seemed embarrassed at the thought of public displays of affection. It just wasn't the Amish way. "Yes, Cheryl." His voice was husky. "We are a team, and I am thankful."

She wanted to say she would solve this by Christmas. She *needed* to do it by Christmas, for Levi, for her, and for the kids. But as the days slipped by, Cheryl knew it would take a Christmas miracle. So instead of making a promise, she reached up and placed her hand on Levi's cheek. "We're in this together, Levi, and we have to remember that God is in it with us too."

Chapter Fourteen

If it wasn't for the feeling of exhaustion, this day would seem like any typical day. The night before, after Cheryl had picked up the kids, they'd come home, decorated cookies, and eaten too many treats before bed. Then this morning, she'd awakened to find that both kids had climbed into bed with her in the night. It would have been perfect if Levi had been there too.

And now Cheryl poured herself coffee as the kids played, and she watched Seth leave after chores. A sinking feeling came over her when she picked the Saturday newspaper up off the front porch. She returned to the table and sat, guessing what she would find on the front page.

Cheryl's fingers trembled as she opened the newspaper. The headline caused her to suck in a breath. LOCAL FARMER FACING CHARGES IN THE CASE OF CRITICALLY INJURED ANGEL.

> *Sugarcreek—*
> *Levi Miller, a farmer in Tuscarawas County, is accused of tampering with a life-size nativity stable structure and bringing great harm to a feuding neighbor. Due to the words shouted between the accused and the victim, and the accused's confession that he was in charge of construction, Levi Miller*

of Sugarcreek was formally arrested and is being held in the county jail until trial. Miller was previously part of the local Amish community until he left the church. He will be represented by the public defender in this matter.

The accident involving Rudy Wight, also from Tuscarawas County, occurred during a live nativity event at Community Bible Church in downtown Sugarcreek. Numerous witnesses spoke of a conflict between the two men at the event, and those close to the victim believe the motivation stemmed from a lawsuit that the victim recently filed against the accused.

Cheryl closed the newspaper, folded it up, and then wrapped her arms around herself, hoping to stop her trembling. Whoever wrote the article was very good at making Levi look bad. They even pointed out that he had left the Amish church. She was just thankful that her name and the Swiss Miss weren't also included in the piece, although she believed both would be added as soon as that information was found out. It was bad enough that Levi's reputation had taken a hit, but she'd hate to think the Swiss Miss would lose income during the busiest time of the year. Income that supported Aunt Mitzi and her mission.

Cheryl's cell phone rang. She retrieved it from the counter and answered it. "Hello?"

"Hi, Cheryl, this is Sarah. I'm so sorry I didn't get back to you right away."

Cheryl stood and paced to the window and watched as Seth's buggy pulled away. She wanted to run to him and ask him to stay—that she didn't know if she could handle this day alone. But instead, she focused on the voice on the phone.

"Sarah, I'm so glad you called back. I was calling for a few reasons." Cheryl decided to talk about the most uncomplicated reason first. "I got a box in the mail from my aunt Mitzi with Christmas presents in it. Aunt Mitzi is so thoughtful. She sent ones for you and Joe. I would love to get together some time to get those to you. I know the kids would love it too."

"Cheryl, that's the last thing I expected to hear you say. I mean, it's very nice that your aunt Mitzi would send us presents. I don't even know if I've met her in person. But you're talking about Christmas presents, and all I can think about is Levi. I know I should have called sooner. But I just now heard about him actually being arrested."

Cheryl moved past the table and the newspaper, refusing to look at the headline again. Instead, she hurried to the living room and sat on the couch to be closer to her children and watch them play as they stacked blocks. She needed their closeness now. "How did you hear? Didn't you leave before it happened?"

"Well, I had a few friends who were there. They texted me. And now it's in the newspaper. Did you know it's in the paper? Everybody knows about Levi's arrest. Joe and I can't believe we just missed seeing the accident. And Joe, well, his friends in law enforcement called him right away."

"They called to talk to Joe about Levi?" Cheryl tried not to sound shocked.

"Cheryl." Sarah gave a nervous chuckle. "Levi is Joe's brother-in-law. It's not every day an officer's brother-in-law gets arrested. They had a lot of questions."

"Well, that's the second reason I called. Have we done something wrong? Maybe something we didn't know about?"

Rebecca looked up at Cheryl, and Cheryl softened her tone. "Joe seemed so upset the other day when we saw you. He seemed like he didn't want you talking to us at all." She forced a smile in Rebecca's direction, and the girl went back to her play.

Sarah laughed, and Cheryl nearly dropped the phone. It wasn't what she had expected at all.

"Cheryl, you're not going to believe this, but Joe didn't recognize you. Not at all. With that hat on, pushed all the way down to your eyebrows, and that big, bulky, dirty coat. He thought you were—"

"Asking for a handout?" Cheryl jumped in.

"Yes, and you know how men are. He didn't even pay much attention to the kids. He said he hasn't been keeping track, and he didn't realize your children were so big. He thought you were a perfect stranger. He was upset with me for telling our business to someone I didn't even know. Can you believe that? He's been worried that if word gets out that we're looking for property, prices will rise, although that seems silly to me."

Cheryl couldn't help but laugh, feeling a huge weight lift off her shoulders. "Oh, I can imagine. I must have really looked quite the mess that day. No makeup at all. Red beanie. Levi's old work coat. I'd been so busy trying to make it out the door, to get to

Levi's nativity program, I wasn't paying attention to how I looked. So I can understand why Joe didn't recognize me at all."

Sarah's voice softened. "I'm so glad that's cleared up."

"But I have to ask…" Cheryl forged ahead with her questions. "What's brought you back to this area?"

"I know this will sound crazy because of the way I ran away from the Amish lifestyle as soon as I turned eighteen. But deep down, I've missed it. I've missed it all these years. Joe thinks we can create a wonderful hobby farm and help people experience the Amish lifestyle."

Cheryl was laughing again. "Oh, great minds must think alike. Years ago, I thought it would be wonderful to host weekends where people lived like the Amish. I thought it would be a huge hit. People are naturally intrigued by a slower pace, a different way of life. I thought they would jump at the chance to spend a long weekend on an Amish farm. Of course, we know that it's not a slow pace."

Sarah chuckled. "Yes, talk to my mother and ask her how relaxing it is to take care of so many people." Then she grew quiet, and Cheryl knew her sister-in-law wanted to ask something. So she waited.

"Listen, I'm just sitting in our small rental, and Joe went out with a friend snowmobiling for the day," Sarah finally said. "Do you mind if I come over? I mean, I enjoy talking to you over the phone, but it would be much better face-to-face."

"I'd love that. Please come. The kids will enjoy it too."

"Okay, good. I'll be right over."

As soon as Cheryl hung up, she looked around her house, and a barrage of disappointment hit her. Yes, it would be good to see Sarah, but what would Sarah think of this place? Cheryl hadn't had a chance to decorate, and she hadn't cleaned in a week. Elizabeth had cleaned the kitchen when she'd been here, but two days without picking up after the kids was as good as twenty, and her living room showed it. But then, in the middle of her thoughts, Cheryl remembered Aunt Mitzi's admonition to always be thankful.

Before she had come to Sugarcreek, Cheryl had been at a bit of a crossroads. Finding herself on the bad end of a failed romance and locked inside a corporate job brought little joy. Aunt Mitzi might have followed her dream to do mission work in Papua New Guinea, but God had brought new goals and dreams to Cheryl's heart in the process. Dreams she was now living, even though it hadn't turned out quite as she had imagined.

Cheryl had jumped at the chance to have a slower-paced lifestyle, although, in reality, it had been hard to get used to. But especially after she married and welcomed children into the family, a slower pace was a thing of the past. If only she could figure out how Naomi did it all so well. She thought about rushing to get everything cleaned up, but she knew that would just get the kids overly excited. So instead, she decided to enjoy a few moments of peace before telling her children they'd soon be having an auntie come over—one they didn't know but who was excited to see them.

Ten minutes later, Rebecca and Matthew were waiting eagerly by the window, squealing with excitement as they watched Sarah pull up. They waved as she parked out front and then hurried up the steps with two gift bags in hand. Rebecca quickly opened the door, and Sarah rushed in with the cold wind.

After the kids were settled, Cheryl invited Sarah to sit down at the table. Then she poured them both a cup of tea.

Cheryl smiled to herself, realizing that Sarah had called Naomi "my mother" when they'd been talking earlier on the phone. But, of course, Naomi was the only mother Sarah had ever known since her biological mother had died on the day she was born.

There was a time that Sarah had pushed Naomi away. It was almost as if she'd been afraid to give her heart to her stepmother, for fear of losing her too. The fact that Sarah and Joe were moving back to the area said a lot. Cheryl wondered if, deep down, Naomi knew how much Sarah cared.

While the children played with the Play-Doh sets that Sarah brought as gifts, Sarah shared some stories with Cheryl of what things had been like when she was a child, and her eyes sparkled as she did.

"Levi was always the best at hide-and-seek. I could never hide well enough to fool him. Although he said it was often my giggles that gave me away." Sarah took a sip of her tea with a smile.

"Has it been hard being out of communication for so long?" Cheryl asked.

Sarah leaned forward as if she had a secret, her long braid resting on the dining room table. "Well, I'm not sure if I'm supposed to tell, but Elizabeth has done an excellent job of keeping me up-to-date on things. She's quite the letter writer, and I'm very familiar with what's happening on the Miller farm. Or should I say the Miller *farms*."

Cheryl nodded, and then she stilled. She was enjoying the time with Sarah and their easy conversation, but something bothered her. Something she'd wanted to know. "Can I ask you something? I've always wondered why you weren't at our wedding, Sarah. I thought maybe you felt bad because your family came to our wedding and not to yours."

"Honestly, things were different when I left. My father and I weren't on good terms. He is stubborn, and so am I. But I think he's softened over time, or at least Elizabeth seems to think so." Sarah watched the children for a few minutes more, and Cheryl waited. She knew there was more that her sister-in-law wanted to say.

"To tell you the truth, even though I was the one who left, I wished that my family would have made more effort to reach out to me. After I heard that Levi was leaving the Amish, I was sure he would call me. I imagined all the conversations we would have— talking about our hearts and following them. I even imagined us chatting about the good things from the Amish that we were thankful for and how we would incorporate them into our own families." Sarah's voice had a wistful tone.

"And Levi never called, did he?"

Sarah shrugged. "No, it was my imagination that got carried away with that one. We both know my brother is not a man of many words." She hesitated again and looked down at her tea. "There's something else I want you to know. I was the one who tried to talk Joe into buying the property next to you and Levi. I had hopes that our relationship could be mended. The problem is that when we saw the price, it was way out of our league. It made me sad because I thought that if we were neighbors, we would have more of a chance to get close."

Cheryl stood up and took two steps toward Sarah, then she bent down and hugged her. "Oh Sarah, you don't have to buy the property next to us for us to grow our relationship. I'm willing to drive fifty miles to do that if I need to. It's just so good to have you in our home. It's so good to have this heart-to-heart talk. We should have done it long ago."

Cheryl returned to her seat. "And just think, it all started by us bumping into each other at that event."

"It started before that. Joe and I have been looking for property around this area since spring. And I should have called. I should have been the one to make an effort to reach out instead of expecting everyone else to reach out to me. Part of it is my pride, I suppose. It's funny how I wanted to run away from the family, the community, the simple life. Yet all those things that made me want to leave are the very things that are now bringing me home."

"Speaking of home." Cheryl poured more hot water into their cups. "My friend Judith said you were here the other day. Or at least from the description she gave I thought it sounded like you."

"Yes, I should have called first, but I lost your number when I lost my last phone. I know I could have called Maam and asked her for your number, but I wasn't ready to see her yet. After I saw you, I told Joe that you and Levi had a dawdy haus. I thought that maybe we could rent it while we were looking for property. But then we saw that you have a friend staying there, and I knew that was no longer an option."

Cheryl laid her hand on Sarah's arm. "Our friend Judith will only be here until the new year. We'd be happy to have you and Joe use the dawdy haus after that for as long as you need it."

Sarah's eyes lit up, but before she could reply the kids ran up and showed off their creations, and soon she left the table to join them. But as much as Cheryl enjoyed watching Sarah interact with her kids, there was one more thing she needed to ask.

"Sarah, I have another question. I hope you don't mind."

Sarah looked up from the floor where she was sitting with Matthew on her lap. "No, not at all. What is it?"

"Why were you talking to Owen Wight? Did that have something to do with wanting his father's property?"

Confusion clouded Sarah's gaze. "Cheryl, what are you talking about?"

"The day of the nativity opening, Joe said you were there to meet someone. I have to admit that I watched you go to the parking lot. It was Owen Wight you were talking to. He's Rudy's son. Rudy, the man who owns the property next to us, was the man who was hurt. He's in critical care in a coma."

Sarah's mouth dropped open, and her eyes blinked slowly as if she was trying to process all that Cheryl was telling her.

"I hope it doesn't sound like I'm accusing you, but there has to be a reason you were meeting Owen."

"We weren't meeting anyone, or at least anyone that we knew." Then, as if a memory resurfaced, Sarah's eyes widened, and she nodded. "Oh yes. I remember now. Joe was meeting with some guy who was buying some of his old baseball cards. We met him in the parking lot. I didn't know his name. I had never seen him before. He was just somebody who had an online shop selling baseball cards. He gave Joe a reasonable price. We had no idea that he was related to the poor man who was hurt."

Heat rose to Cheryl's cheeks, and she couldn't meet Sarah's gaze.

"Cheryl, is something wrong?"

She had a decision to make. She could steer their conversation in another direction, or she could tell the truth. She'd learned over the years that telling the truth was always the right thing, but she didn't want to hurt Sarah's feelings, especially when they were trying to build their relationship after all these years.

"Cheryl, is everything all right?" Sarah asked again.

"Well, my mind has been working double-time trying to figure everything out. First, the way Owen acted was strange, and then when I saw you both meeting him, I guessed it was because you wanted the property. So I thought that maybe Joe and Owen were trying to figure out how Joe could buy their place and, well, I'm very good at making up all types of stories in my mind."

Sarah nodded slowly, and then her eyes grew wide. "Are you saying that you thought Joe and Owen were working together to get Rudy 'out of the way' so we could get their place?" Sarah used air quotes and, with a laugh, Matthew mimicked her.

Cheryl nodded and then covered her face. "Sadly, yes," she said, peeking between two fingers.

"Oh, but you don't think that anymore, do you? Please tell me that you don't associate Joe with any wrongdoing." Sarah winked.

"I mean, we would love the property next to you, but it's nothing that we could afford. We were looking at a much smaller two-acre piece of land about a mile down the road. And that's why Joe is selling his baseball cards. We worked hard to get out of debt, and now we've been selling things off here and there to build up a down payment. After accumulating so much debt during our marriage, I now know why my parents insisted on not buying anything until they had the cash. A load of debt is a big burden to carry."

"Yes," Cheryl agreed. "I've learned so many good things from the Amish. Having less isn't about missing out at all. It's about having the freedom to do more."

"Freedom is key. We have so many dreams. They sort of sound crazy when you say them out loud. Joe's been wanting to get out of law enforcement for a while. It was hard to be on the streets, so he decided to be a detective, but that was hard too. He never liked to tell me what he was investigating, but I watch the news, and I could imagine. When they told him he was doing such a good job that they would promote him to the head of the department, he had to stop and think about it. He didn't want to be in charge of everyone and everything. He was already gone from home so much, I told him that I didn't care if we had to build an igloo on my parents' farm, I wanted him to quit. Thankfully, he agreed."

"So now you're going to come here and provide an Amish experience?" Cheryl realized this wasn't a joke. Sarah was serious.

"Well, it's Joe's idea, but I would love to have a hobby farm. We could even hire local Amish youth to put on demonstrations in the summer for tourists. Joe jokingly calls it an Amish tourist trap, but that makes it sound like he's in it just for the money. Believe it or not, he thinks something like this could benefit the local Amish and tourists. He has excellent ideas."

"I bet Levi would love to talk to Joe about those ideas." Cheryl forced a smile. "We just have to figure out how to get him home."

She rose and walked to the back window overlooking the barn. "It looks like a storm's coming in," she said more to herself than to Sarah.

Sarah jumped to her feet. "Oh, I need to get going before it does. Joe doesn't trust me to drive on snowy roads—at least in a car. I've convinced him I can do a mighty fine job in a horse and buggy though."

Sarah said goodbye to the kids, and then she bundled up. Cheryl was about to get the presents from Aunt Mitzi when Sarah waved a hand in her direction. "No, leave them here. Then we have an excuse to come for Christmas," she said with a smile.

"We would love that," Cheryl said, emphasizing the *we*.

Yes, Levi has to be home. He just has to be.

Cheryl stepped outside to walk Sarah to the car. A brisk wind blew, shaking the afternoon snow off the trees. Then Cheryl watched Sarah's car back out, leaving twin tracks on the snow. And as Sarah turned from their driveway to the main road, Cheryl saw the same woman again.

She had parked her white truck out there and was again snapping shots of the Wight farm with her camera. Cheryl hurried inside to get her phone to call Chief Twitchell, but the young woman was gone by the time she got back to the window. Instead of calling for the chief, Cheryl set her phone down. While the afternoon had helped her to take Joe and Sarah off her list of suspects, seeing that young woman again just moved her to the top of the list. Whoever she was.

"I need to watch at this time tomorrow," Cheryl said to herself. "There has to be something I've missed. Something happening with that woman." She just had to know what it was about.

CHAPTER FIFTEEN

Sunday morning dawned beautifully. The night before, Cheryl had decided that they would stay home from church. She didn't know if she would be able to handle all the questions. Or how her kids would respond to being the center of attention for all the wrong reasons.

Since the Amish church only met twice a month and this was an off week, Naomi and Seth said they would come for the day. Seth was coming over to do the chores anyway, and Naomi said she'd be delighted to join him.

Peering out into the sun-kissed morning, Cheryl noticed that more snow had fallen in the night. A white blanket stretched over the fields, hiding December's corn stubble. Piles of snow looked like whipped cream, covering the mounds of haystacks next to the barn. With its gable roof, the large red barn was a spot of color in the white landscape.

Even though it would have been the perfect morning to relax with a cup of hot cocoa in front of the fire, Cheryl hadn't been able to sleep, so she'd gotten up early to do some searching on her phone. She was thankful that she had learned how to look things up on public records. It took a while, but she found the information about the company that had wanted to buy the Wight farm. She longed to share what she found with Naomi. Still, she waited until Seth had done the chores, they'd enjoyed a big breakfast together, and they'd settled down with coffee while the children occupied themselves with cartoons. Then she shared the new information.

"It looks as if the original buyer who withdrew their offer was a large company. They were planning on turning Rudy's property into a subdivision."

Naomi had brought her knitting along with her, and her hands moved in a blur as she worked on scarves for Christmas. "A subdivision. Land's sake. That would have changed everything, wouldn't it?"

"Yes, and I'm thankful that it didn't go through." Cheryl scrolled through the document on her phone and then paused. She sat up straighter in her chair. "Look at this. The date that the property was unlisted was before Levi cut down the tree limbs. Since that's the case, it's not possible that Levi cutting down the limbs had anything to do with the sale of the property falling through."

Seth settled into the chair next to his wife with a cup of coffee. "From what Levi shared with me, the Realtor claimed it was the cutting of the limbs that stopped the sale."

Cheryl nodded. "I found out the same thing from him—his name is Rich Chetty."

Seth took a sip of his coffee before saying, "Have you talked to Rudy's lawyer? I know Levi went to see him. He might have some information."

Cheryl's eyes widened. "What do you mean? Who is Rudy's lawyer? And how come I didn't know about this before?"

"His name is Todd Arnold. Remember a few weeks ago when Levi went in to talk to him?"

A foggy memory filtered through Cheryl's mind. She remembered Levi mentioning it while she made breakfast. He said he had to go into town to speak to someone about their property. At least she thought it had been about their property.

"I think I remember. Levi said there were some questions about the property line. It's sort of fuzzy because Rebecca was crying, saying her head hurt." She turned to Naomi. "That was the day you came over to watch Matthew, wasn't it? And we found out Rebecca had that sinus infection."

Naomi paused her knitting. "Yes, I remember. And I also remember Levi talking to Seth, mentioning problems with the limbs over the property line."

Cheryl rose and paced, and she wondered how, with all the late nights she'd spent trying to look at every angle of Levi's arrest, she hadn't remembered that he'd gone to talk to a lawyer.

She stopped her pacing and turned to her in-laws. "This makes things look even worse, doesn't it? The fact that Rudy had a case against Levi. He did have a case, didn't he?"

"Yes." Seth set his coffee mug down and leaned forward in his chair, resting his arms on his legs. Cheryl sat across from him, and Seth narrowed his gaze on her. "Rudy's lawyer filed a damage claim against Levi. The man insisted that Levi owes Rudy a large sum of money."

It was motive. Yet another thing that directly pointed to Levi.

Cheryl placed a hand over her heart and pressed, as if doing so could take away the ache that was there. Thinking back, there were a couple of times a few weeks ago that Levi had tried to talk to her. She remembered that just as Rebecca started feeling better, Matthew got sick.

"I feel like such a horrible wife. Levi tried to talk to me about this problem. Once, when he was talking about cutting down tree limbs, I'm pretty sure I fell asleep right there on the couch." She pressed her hand to her forehead. "I should have caught on that it was something serious, since he kept bringing it up. I just had no idea that a damage claim had been filed against him recently. Whatever for?"

"Well, the lawyer can give you more details, but from what I remember, Rudy put his property up for sale a few months back," Seth said. "Around the same time, Levi discovered that the line of trees leading down Rudy's driveway hung over onto your property. The branches and leaves were cluttering up the creek, which runs from your spring, and they were blocking the water from getting into the fields."

"I do remember Levi talking about that," Naomi added. "He had to cut off a whole bunch of branches so they would not block the creek. Not doing so would have put his livestock at risk."

Cheryl perked up, turning to Seth. "But like I just mentioned, the public records show that the property was unlisted *before* Levi cut down any trees, so that couldn't have affected the sale at all."

Naomi clucked her tongue. "Unless it was unlisted because Rudy knew he would get more money by doing a for sale by owner. Maybe he heard of an Amish family who wanted to buy his farm."

Cheryl sank into her chair once more. "But still, how could cutting some limbs hinder a sale like that?"

Seth shrugged. "I am not an expert, but have you gone to look at those trees? Really look at the eyesore they have become? That is one of the joys of driving by buggy—I have a chance to look everything over real good. When Levi removed those limbs, it changed the look of the trees leading into Rudy's property, especially with a whole line of trees missing half of their branches all on the same side."

"But if Rudy never responded to Levi when Levi told him that he needed a solution, Levi did what he had the legal right to do, correct?" Cheryl asked.

Seth shrugged. "Ja, of course, but that does not mean that Rudy was not upset."

Cheryl nodded. "Yes, he was so angry and red-faced right before the program started. You should have seen the way he yelled at Levi, making so many accusations."

They sat there for a few minutes, each one lost in thought. The cartoon on the television played a happy song, and the kids sang along, but Cheryl felt anything but happy.

After a few minutes, she turned to Seth, thankful for his wisdom and his help. "Thank you, Seth, for reminding me of Rudy's lawyer. Instead of speculating any further, I think I need to talk to him. I'll see if I can do it first thing in the morning."

"I will go with you," Naomi volunteered. Then she turned to her husband. "Seth, you don't mind staying with the children after doing the chores, do you?"

Seth chuckled. "I do not mind. As long as there are animals in the barn to look at, we will be fine."

"Naomi, that's kind of you, but you don't need to go with me. You are so busy around your place, especially with Christmas."

"Nonsense. You know as well as I that Elizabeth is very capable of taking care of things when I am gone. You and I have been partners, so to speak, for a while, and I always love a good interrogation."

Seth let out a heavy sigh. "As much as I do not think you two need to always poke your noses into things, I do think it is a good idea that you talk to this lawyer. It seems logical that Rudy's anger had to do with what happened to those trees. This information, more than anything, could be what we need to get Levi back home where he belongs."

They sat there a few minutes more, and Naomi scratched her head. "I know I should let it drop, but there is still something about this that does not make sense."

"And what's that?" Cheryl focused intently on her mother-in-law.

"Rudy has been your neighbor for many years, and it seems that there has always been good communication before. If Levi tried to reach out to Rudy, why didn't he respond?"

"I don't understand that either," Cheryl agreed. "After all these years, why would there be trouble between the two of them now? They have always gotten along so well before. So what happened? You're right, it doesn't make sense."

Seth cleared his throat. "The best thing would be that Rudy gets well enough that he comes out of that coma so we can ask him."

"In the meantime, we still need to remember to pray for him," Naomi said. "Unfortunately, someone made a plan to hurt him. And that means there is more trouble in his life than we may have initially realized. People are good at hiding a lot of things. And I have found, over the years, that the things they try to hide the most are the troubles they are in. For a while they may try to figure it out themselves. After that, they may try to make everything right. And when that does not work, it is a good time to step in. To offer the love and the grace that they need."

Cheryl pulled a blanket from the back of the sofa and wrapped it around her shoulders. "Levi is a wonderful person to talk to. He has a lot of wisdom. And I think I know where he got it from."

Naomi laughed. "It must be from Seth. I have made plenty of mistakes. When it came to raising that boy, I often shook my head when he did things at his own pace. But I have come to see that even as Levi is busy at work, he is noticing the people around him. He is doing what he can to support others. And that is what makes it so hard to see the position that he is in now. But I have a feeling that God is going to use him there too. God always surprises us by placing silver linings even around the darkest storm clouds."

"Sometimes I feel like I should just follow you around. If I wrote down all the wise things you say, I think that, pretty soon, we'd have enough for one of those daily wisdom calendars."

Naomi laughed. "Well, when you've lived as long as I have, you learn a few things. So I hope that something I say once in a while makes sense. More than that, I'm happy to help you."

CHAPTER SIXTEEN

Cheryl was thankful to have Naomi by her side the following day as they entered the office of Todd Arnold. While no one would ever ask Naomi to be a bodyguard, it was good to have her there as a peaceful presence.

The office was in one of the historic buildings in Sugarcreek. The worn wooden floor looked original. Inside the front entryway were two doorways and a staircase, leading off the main landing. Only one of the doors was marked. A brass plaque hung over the thick wooden door and read LAW OFFICE.

Cheryl looked at Naomi and lifted an eyebrow. "Do we knock or just go in?"

"I would say knock."

Cheryl lifted her hand and knocked loudly. She paused and didn't hear anything, so she knocked again. This time she heard footsteps and took a step back. The door opened with a creak, and Cheryl sucked in a gasp.

"You!" she said. It was the man who had been watching her in the Swiss Miss the day after Rudy's accident.

The tall, stocky man with light brown hair and wire-rimmed glasses eyed her from the doorway.

"Mrs. Miller, what a surprise." He wore a suit that had seen better days. It was open in the front, and his white shirt underneath looked dingy.

"How do you know my name?" Cheryl asked as she felt Naomi grip her elbow.

"When I met your husband he said you managed the Swiss Miss. I've seen you there before." He took a step back and gestured them inside. "Won't you come in?"

His smile was plastic, but he didn't appear dangerous. Cheryl peered behind him at the sparsely decorated office. There was a secretary's desk and a waiting area with a sofa. A light blue and white rug covered most of the floor, and a dark hallway extended beyond that.

"I'm sorry, but my secretary is out of town." He waved his hand again. "I assume you've come to talk about the lawsuit?"

"Yes, I have. We have." Cheryl hurried into the office and motioned for Naomi to follow her. She moved to sit in the waiting area, but Mr. Arnold cleared his throat, so she paused.

"My office is my preference, if you don't mind." He moved in the direction of the hallway and flipped on a light. Cheryl and Naomi followed him to the first door on the left.

Inside the spacious office, Mr. Arnold walked to his desk in a slow, steady gait as if he didn't have a care in the world. Goose bumps rose on Cheryl's arms as she remembered what Rich Chetty had said about Rudy Wight having light brown hair and wire-rimmed glasses. She knew she wouldn't focus on anything else that Mr. Arnold said if she didn't ask about that first. Why had he claimed to be someone else? Cheryl sat on one of the two chairs in front of the desk and folded her hands on her lap. Naomi sat beside her.

"Mr. Arnold, I do want to ask about the lawsuit, but first I need to know, have you ever worked with Sugarcreek Realty?"

"Mrs. Miller, if you're asking that question then you know I have, as a representative for Mr. Wight."

"I thought so, but when I was talking to Rich Chetty yesterday, he described Mr. Wight as having light brown hair and wire-rimmed glasses. He described you."

"Ma'am, as a representative for Mr. Wight, I visited the realty office twice, and both times I mentioned that I *represented* Mr. Wight. I never said I was him." Mr. Arnold leaned back in his chair, rested his elbows on the armrests, and steepled his fingers in front of his chin. "If you've met Mr. Chetty you know he is an anxious sort of person and easily confused."

She crossed one leg over the other, feeling her own anxiety rise in this man's presence. "Well, I don't know—"

"Cheryl," Naomi interrupted, "perhaps we should simply stick to the real reason for our visit today."

Cheryl turned and eyed Naomi. From Naomi's lifted eyebrows, she could tell that her mother-in-law did not believe this man either. But she was wise enough to move Cheryl toward the conversation that mattered.

She turned back to the lawyer. "Yes, of course. Mr. Arnold, I'm here seeking information about the lawsuit that our neighbor Mr. Wight has against my husband."

The man turned and opened a drawer in a file cabinet behind him. He flipped through the labeled green files and pulled out a red folder.

Cheryl waited patiently as he read through the file. Finally, after a few minutes, he closed it and looked up at her.

"Well, looking through this file, I see that your name is also listed on the property. The Miller Farm is owned by Levi and Cheryl Miller. So in that case, Mr. Wight's claim is against you too."

Cheryl straightened in her chair. "So you're saying there's a claim against me?"

"Yes, and this is serious. I'm sorry to deliver this news, but your husband's actions caused Mr. Wight's trees to be damaged. More than that, it caused him to lose out on the sale of his property. I'm afraid that your husband owes Mr. Wight a large sum of money."

Cheryl felt Naomi stiffen in the chair beside her. Even though Mr. Arnold said he was sorry to deliver that news, the smirk on his face said he was anything but.

"May I have a copy of the paperwork? I'd like to read the details for myself."

"I can give you a copy, but there will be a fee. Your husband already had the papers delivered to him. Maybe you could ask him where they are."

Cheryl narrowed her gaze. He knew she had limited opportunities to talk to Levi and the reason why. But she could also tell it would be no use to try to change the man's mind. "Yes, of course."

Mr. Arnold stared at her without concern or emotion. "Of course, even if you did want to pay the fee, my assistant is in

Nebraska visiting her parents. So the soonest I could get a copy to you would be after the New Year."

"Don't worry yourself—or your assistant, Mr. Arnold. I'll see what I can do."

Cheryl stood, and beside her Naomi did the same.

Moving toward the door, Cheryl paused and turned back to the man. "Oh, I do have one more question. Did you get all your Christmas cards sent out, the ones you purchased at the Swiss Miss the day after the accident? I find it so strange that I hadn't seen you in my store before, yet there you were, the day after your client was seriously injured."

"Please don't flatter yourself, Mrs. Miller. First, I haven't lived in Sugarcreek very long. I've yet to visit most of the local stores. And second, those cards were for my mother. Sending out Christmas cards is more her thing than mine. It's just a waste of money, in my opinion."

Cheryl released a sigh of exasperation. Why did this lawyer have to be so frustrating?

With a final thanks, the women left the office and hurried to the car. Thankfully, they had a visit with Levi to look forward to. Finally, finally, he would be able to give Cheryl the information that Todd Arnold refused to provide. Yet even more than getting the information, Cheryl needed to see her husband's smile and the loving look he always cast in her direction that said, *Everything's going to be okay.*

CHAPTER SEVENTEEN

Nothing about this day had gone as planned. Cheryl slumped onto the couch and kicked off her shoes. After visiting Todd Arnold's office, she and Naomi stopped by to see Levi. Unfortunately, when they got there, a notice was posted on the door of the police station. An illness had broken out among the prisoners, and they and some of the staff were under quarantine. From the car, Cheryl called the station. She was told prisoners could only take phone calls during certain daytime hours, and those hours had passed.

Poor Levi. She couldn't even call to tell him she was sorry for not paying better attention all the times he'd tried to tell her what had been happening with the creek, the trees, the property line, and the legal action that was taken against him—against them.

After Cheryl dropped Naomi off, she came home to a note from Seth saying that he'd taken the kids on a sleigh ride and they'd be back before afternoon chores. With all that was going wrong, at least her children had family members to care for them.

A knock sounded at the door, and Cheryl opened it to find Judith smiling with a large pie dish in her hand. "Apple pie for your dessert. You just need to bake it at 350 for forty-five minutes. Is it all right if I bring it in and put it in your refrigerator?"

"Yes, please come in."

Cheryl knew she was poor company right now. "I'm so sorry. I'm not very talkative." She explained to her friend about the visit with the lawyer and the quarantine at the Sugarcreek police station.

"I'd be worried if you were happy and chatty. I know it's giving you a lot to think about." Judith placed the pie in the fridge, and Cheryl gave her a hug of thanks.

"I just wish I had listened better to Levi when I had the chance. Maybe we wouldn't be in this mess at all."

Judith sat at the kitchen table, pushing aside scattered peas from what Cheryl assumed was the kids' lunch. "You'll be able to talk to him tomorrow, won't you? Then you can ask him where he put the paperwork. I'm sure being able to read it for yourself will be a big help."

Cheryl plopped in the chair closest to her. "Yes, of course, but how will I sleep tonight?" She would have placed her head on the table for emphasis, but more peas were smashed on the table in that spot too.

Judith sat up straighter and pointed a finger into the air. "You'll be able to sleep tonight because you'll find the answers before you go to bed."

"I will, will I? I still have dinner to cook, the kitchen to clean, and the laundry needs to get done. I don't think that Matthew has any clean shirts and—"

"And I am very good at both cooking and laundry. I have some carrots, celery, and frozen chicken breasts. If you have some noodles, I can make some chicken noodle soup."

"And what will I be doing?"

"Well, if the lawyer served Levi papers, he probably stashed them in the house somewhere. You can do a little sleuthing. And I'll stay out of your way too. I'll grab your noodles and a basket of laundry and take it to my place."

"Judith, I can't even imagine what I'd be doing right now if I didn't have you. You give me the best ideas, and you care for me." Cheryl pointed at her. "I'm thinking you really don't want to go back to Arizona and miss all this excitement, do you?"

"Oh, I'm going back to Arizona, but I'll be back to visit often. You and Levi and the children have become like a second family to me, and family sticks together, right?"

"Right. God knew what He was doing when he brought you to me."

Within a few minutes, Cheryl found the noodles Judith needed. Judith took them and a large basket of laundry and carried both to the dawdy haus.

Cheryl sat in her favorite chair to think, and immediately Beau jumped into her lap. "Okay, Beau, it's just you and me again. At least for a little while." She stroked the length of the cat's soft fur and felt herself settling to his purr. "If you were Levi, where would you put important papers?"

Beau looked at her and blinked slowly.

"You have no idea either, do you?"

She continued to pet Beau as she thought about every area of her home. They had a small desk, but it was filled with the paperwork she brought home from the store and Rebecca's craft supplies. Levi's dresser was empty except for clothes, and she knew every inch of their closet and what was in it. Where could he have put important paperwork like that?

Then Cheryl remembered where Levi kept things that he didn't want the kids to get into. He didn't have an office of his own, but there was a corner in his shop where he kept important papers, like vaccination records for his cattle, his truck registration, and other items of the sort.

"Well, Beau, it's worth a shot. It's the only place I can think of." Cheryl lifted Beau off her lap and placed him on the couch. He looked at her with disapproval and let out a meow of protest. "I know, I know. I'm sorry I'm getting up so soon." She stroked his back one more time. "You miss when you had my lap all to yourself every evening, don't you?"

Cheryl dressed in her boots, coat, and hat again. She knew that if Levi had been served papers, he wouldn't have tried to keep them from her on purpose. He would have set them aside until the time was right—when they had some quiet time together to talk. But, unfortunately, with their busy household, that time hadn't come.

It was cold outside. Long pointy icicles hung along the gutters, and Cheryl's breath came out in white puffs as she hurried to Levi's shop. The air inside smelled like motor oil, dust, and cold cement. She stepped around two old tires and walked past a workbench covered with boxes of screws and washers, various tools, cans of grease, and seed bags. Instead of staying out in the cold to go through the thick stack of papers, Cheryl picked up the whole pile and carried it into the house. Within a few minutes, she sat on the couch again with the documents on the floor near her feet.

As Beau eyed her from the chair, she made neat piles on the coffee table in front of her. There were more papers than she had expected, and this was something she should have done a while ago.

While Levi was a wonderful man who always did a fine job taking care of her and the kids, he was not the type of person who liked to sit down and work at a desk. The more papers she sorted through, the more she saw he had no filing system.

Soon piles for various categories developed. There were stacks of papers they needed for their home and vehicles. There were invoices for bills paid in full. There were papers for their many animals, including sale notes. Cheryl also created a pile of papers she was sure could be thrown away, but she didn't want to do that until she asked Levi. And finally, in the middle of the stack, Cheryl found a large manila envelope. The return address was Todd Arnold, Lawyer, Sugarcreek. She set it aside and continued sorting the papers, hoping to find anything else that would answer any questions about Rudy and Levi's relationship.

When she was done sorting, Cheryl picked up the papers she thought could be thrown away and put them into a plastic bag. As she did, one fell to the ground. She paused, realizing that a letter written in Levi's hand had been inside a larger envelope that had first appeared to be empty. Cheryl unfolded the letter and began to read.

Dear Rudy,
I know we have been neighbors for many years, and I am sorry that things have turned out as they currently are. In October and November I visited your home at least ten times.

I talked to either your son or your wife each time, telling them that I needed to speak with you about the limbs overhanging the creek.

Dead limbs and leaves have been falling from those trees for four years, and the more the tree limbs have stretched over to my side of the property line, the more problems they have caused. Finally, it came to the point that there was so much debris, I spent nearly a whole week cleaning the creek just so that my livestock could get the water they needed. The problem is, with those branches continuing to hang over my side, they would cause the same issue very soon. And I could not put my livestock at risk like that.

After many weeks of waiting to hear back from you, I knew I had to take action. I talked to someone from town who understands property laws, and he gave me good advice. He showed me the code that says that any tree limbs hanging over the property line onto my side can be cut away, especially if they are causing damage. So, after numerous attempts to reach you, I did what I had to do, which was legally in my right. Still, I am sorry if any of my actions have caused your family trouble. I do not want there to be bad feelings between us.

Your friend,

Levi

Cheryl set the letter down. Her heart swelled with love for her husband. How did she deserve such a wonderful man? As far as she could tell, Levi had done everything according to the law. Yet he still had compassion for others. Cheryl looked at the letter's date. She gasped to see that it had been written only two days before the accident. So amid his busy week, Levi had paused long enough to try to make things right with Rudy. With all he'd been doing to work on the nativity set, he had taken the time to write a letter and make a photocopy of it.

When Cheryl had found a box for all her neat piles, she opened up the envelope from Todd Arnold. Anger surged within her when she saw the amount of the lawsuit. As she read, she discovered that Mr. Arnold was acting on behalf of Rudy Wight for damages done to his property, which led to a profitable sale falling through. As Cheryl read, all she could think was, *Lies, lies, lies!*

The good news was that now she had the facts to prove that nothing Levi had done had stopped the sale. The bad news was that even if she took all her newfound evidence with her to the police, that still didn't help Levi's current situation.

The only thing that could be proven was that Rudy Wight was suing Levi for a considerable amount—one that could put the Miller farm in jeopardy. And for any jury, she supposed that could give Levi a reason for why he'd want to hurt their neighbor. So, yes, Cheryl had found helpful information, but what she had discovered would help the police officers establish motive too.

She assumed that Levi had mailed the letter. So the question was, did Rudy receive it? And if he received it, did it make a difference? Did Rudy see it for the peace offering that Levi meant it to be? Or did it fuel his anger? Was the letter what they were fighting about at the church?

Maybe soon she'd have answers to those questions. Then, hopefully, she would be able to call and have the chance to talk to Levi. She had so many questions to ask. She also had many apologies to give.

It pained her to know that in the middle of all this trouble, Levi had to carry it on his own. She made a promise to herself that no matter how busy she was, she would take time for her husband. She would take time to listen and pay attention. Things would not slow down anytime soon with a busy store to run and two active kids. But the difference would be where she chose to focus.

Cheryl tromped through the snow and smiled grimly to herself as she headed to the dawdy haus to tell Judith what she'd found. She'd hoped to get more answers today, but that hadn't happened.

Yet by talking to various people on her quest, Cheryl discovered that she wasn't the only one struggling this Christmas. While beautiful decorations brought beauty to Sugarcreek, there were those inside the walls of the buildings and homes who weren't having the type of Christmas they had wished for either.

"Do you need help tomorrow?" Judith asked, welcoming Cheryl into the dawdy haus that smelled of warm soup and laundry soap.

"Do you have time? You've done so much already. I hate to ask."

"You're not asking. I'm offering. There's a difference."

"Esther left a message on my phone today. She said the Swiss Miss has been extra busy. She also had a problem with one of our suppliers, and double the number of fresh wreaths we ordered was delivered. I need to figure that out, because that's an expense we weren't planning on. And if you don't mind helping customers…"

Judith clapped her hands. "It sounds like fun. I'll be there bright and early."

"I'll stop by too, to check on things. Thank you so much. I honestly don't know what I would do without you."

"You may have mentioned that," Judith said with a wink. "I'm glad I can be here, thrilled to help. Remember, there are many seasons of our lives. Some seasons require us to give, but sometimes the harder seasons are when we must accept help."

Judith's words stayed in Cheryl's mind long after the older woman helped carry the laundry and the soup back to the house. Her words were true. Cheryl often found it easier to give help. But this week she'd sure gotten a lot of practice receiving it.

Chapter Eighteen

Judith's smile was the first thing that greeted Cheryl as she entered the Swiss Miss. Then the sights and sounds of Christmas and the aroma of cinnamon, apple spice, and citrus filled her senses. The older woman was holding up two red and green patterned aprons for a customer to view.

"Cheryl, so good to see you. I stopped at the Honey Bee and picked up a hot tea and scone for you. I know with so much going on you haven't taken time for yourself, so I put it in your office." Judith's white hair was perfectly styled, and Cheryl noticed that she was even wearing a touch of makeup. She wore a sweatshirt that read, Most likely to be on the NICE list, which Cheryl had to agree was true.

"Thank you, Judith. Do you know what I love about you? You not only think of others. You also act."

"Cheryl, I'm so glad you're here." Lydia hurried out from the back room. "I got a hold of the tree farm. They said they had a hiccup in their system, and the order went through twice, so they said to keep the extra wreaths and greenery, no charge." Lydia chuckled. "They said neither would be very fresh by the time we shipped them back."

Cheryl unzipped her jacket. "Well, that's very nice of them, but what are we going to do with all of it?" She glanced around the store. There wasn't an inch of extra space. "It'll be horrible if we can't put it to good use."

Then an image filled Cheryl's mind. It was the bare office of Sugarcreek Realty. Even though there were things that she needed to get done today, she thought of something Aunt Mitzi had said. *"It's always the right time to do the right thing."*

Cheryl zipped her coat back up. "Actually, Lydia, I know just the right place to take some of those wreaths and greenery. Judith, can you help?"

"Sure. Does it have something to do with blessing someone in our community?" A sparkle lit in Judith's eyes.

"Yes. I have an idea for giving a bit of the extra to someone who really could use cheering up."

The two women went to the back room and found the decorations. Cheryl scanned the shelves of the storeroom and located wire-rimmed ribbon. She handed some to Judith, and they both set to work adding special touches to the greenery. Cheryl also retrieved a Christmas card from the card rack.

The wreaths and swags looked beautiful by the time Cheryl and Judith finished fixing them up. Then they hurried down to Sugarcreek Realty.

Cheryl peered inside the window and saw Rich Chetty sitting at his desk with a stack of papers beside him. A forlorn expression was on his face. He turned with curiosity when Cheryl knocked.

If it was possible, the front office looked even more tired than it did the day before. Cheryl entered with a wreath in one arm and a pine swag in the other. Judith followed.

"I'm sorry, but you must have the wrong place," he called to them. For the first time, Cheryl noticed a photo of a young girl and boy on his desk, about the same ages as Rebecca and Matthew. She knew that later she would ask Judith to find a few special things for Rich's kids from the Swiss Miss. But for now, she hoped the greenery would brighten his office and his day.

Cheryl walked to his desk and laid the wreath on it. "This is the right place, and I've come with a few things for you, Mr. Chetty."

The man's eyes widened in surprise. "I don't understand. What's going on? I don't have the money to pay for all that. I can't afford it. Not this year."

"I'm sorry I didn't give you all the details the other day right from the start. But my husband is Levi Miller. He's the one who cut down the tree limbs." Cheryl thought about saying more, especially how she knew that it wasn't Levi's actions that stopped the sale of the property, but she decided not to. Justifying her husband's actions wasn't why she'd come. She'd come to spread a bit of joy.

"I'm sorry you're having a hard Christmas," she continued, "and I would like to make it just a little better for you."

She hadn't eliminated him as a suspect, but something in her gut told her that this man—as desperate as he was—wasn't the one who'd sabotaged the platform to hurt Rudy.

Mr. Chetty's face grew red. "Well, I—I don't know—uh… How could you come back here knowing that what your husband did ruined, well, everything?"

"I know what you think, but I also know that if I were to hold a grudge against you for believing my husband made the sale fall through, it would say more about me than about you. These are gifts for you, and with your permission, my friend and I would love to decorate your office."

Judith nodded her approval. "Please, would you let us?"

Cheryl put an envelope on his desk. "My husband, Levi, is a generous man, Mr. Chetty. It would hurt him to know that there are those in our community who come to this Christmas season with limited resources. So we'd like to help you out, if you'll let us. It's not much, but I hope you can do something special for your family."

Cheryl hadn't known what to expect, but the man settled back in his seat and covered his face with his hands. "I'm sorry I said those things against your husband." He rubbed his face and looked up at her. "I know those tree limbs had nothing to do with the sale falling through. Mr. Wight sent me an email and said that even though he was upset about the limbs, he had personal reasons for taking the property off the market." Mr. Chetty shrugged. "It's just easier to pick a scapegoat sometimes, you know?" He fiddled with one of the ribbons on the wreath. "I don't know what to say except thank you."

Cheryl and Judith set to work decorating the office. Twenty minutes later, the place had been transformed into a festive atmosphere. And as Cheryl and Judith were leaving, they noticed that a few window shoppers had stepped inside and were looking at the properties on the bulletin board. But the best result of their work was Mr. Chetty's beaming face.

Cheryl and Judith strolled away, side by side, and Cheryl's shoulder bumped Judith's. "Now, this is the start of a good day."

"I agree. Did you see his face as we worked? It was like a kid at Christmas!" Judith released a hearty laugh.

Cheryl thought again of how it wasn't easy to accept help. She'd received a lot lately, and it felt wonderful to be on the giving end.

"This is how I feel every time you let me serve you." Judith smiled, almost as if reading Cheryl's mind. "I believe God set it up like that. We find joy to give and to see others receive."

When they arrived back at the Swiss Miss, Lydia and Esther were still busy up front, and Judith eagerly jumped in to join them. Then, with a smile and an extra hop in her step, Cheryl walked to her office. She laughed out loud when she saw the scone and the tea still waiting. She'd been so busy spreading cheer that she'd forgotten about the gift she'd been given.

She sat down and took a sip from the paper cup. The tea had cooled off but tasted good all the same. She took a bite of the scone, savoring the almond and cranberry flavor. Cheryl enjoyed every bit and then looked at the list she'd made the night Naomi and Seth took the kids. Most of her questions still needed to be answered, and something deep in her gut told her that something had to happen soon. Between her and the police asking questions, there had to be someone who knew something.

As those thoughts filled her mind, another idea popped to the top. *God knows.*

Cheryl pushed the last corner of the scone to the side and bowed her head. "Dear God, You know how hard I've been working. You know how much I love my husband. How much I believe in him. I have been trying so hard, and it seems like no matter what I discover, it leads to a dead end. But the truth is that Christmas is about You. This whole season is about You, Lord. I've wanted it to be about justice for Levi. I have been making it about bringing him home. And I still want that more than anything. But help me to remember that You are the Lord of the season. Help me to give love and show love, even when I can't get answers."

After praying, Cheryl finished up a small pile of paperwork, and at the appropriate time, she called the county jail.

"I'm sorry, ma'am," the female officer said. "The quarantine has been extended, and we aren't having the prisoners leave their cells at this time, not even for calls. But you can call back tomorrow and try again." Defensiveness was evident in her tone.

Cheryl dropped her head and closed her eyes, knowing it wasn't this woman's fault. "I'm sorry you have to face this, especially at Christmas. I'll try again tomorrow, thank you."

The line was silent, and for a moment Cheryl wondered if the call had dropped.

"Hello?" Cheryl said. "Are you still there?"

"Yes, I just don't know what to say. Every other caller has yelled at me. Thank you."

"You're welcome. I'll talk to you tomorrow."

Disappointed that she couldn't talk to Levi, Cheryl had a long-ing to see her kids. With a forced smile, she told the others she was leaving. All of them waved her out to her car and told her they would take care of things. She knew they would.

Cheryl was almost to her vehicle when the crunch of snow behind her caught her attention. Fear pricked her heart and caused the hair to rise on the back of her neck. She turned quickly and spotted a man standing there, his arm stretched toward her. Cheryl let out a squeal, then covered her mouth when she recognized Rich Chetty.

"Oh, it's you."

Mr. Chetty's words rushed out. "I'm so sorry to scare you. I—I just wanted to say, uh, thank you again. I didn't expect that."

Cheryl started to explain that she had extra wreaths, and it was no problem, but she kept that to herself. She wanted Mr. Chetty to know that she had thought of him, and it was a gift.

"You're welcome. I'm glad it brought you joy."

He cleared his throat, looked to his boots, and then up to her face again. "I, uh, also wanted to tell you that I'm sorry about your husband. I already called the police department."

Confusion clouded Cheryl's mind. "You called the police department? Why?"

He shrugged. "Well, I thought I should tell them what I knew. I read about his arrest, and I know a bit about the feud the paper spoke of. They connected me with Chief Twitchell, and I told him that Mr. Wight had emailed me and stopped the sale even before your husband cut down those limbs." He shuffled his feet and gave a weak smile. "I—I just thought you should know."

She pressed her gloved hands against her cheeks and smiled. "Thank you, that means a lot."

"The chief is coming by tomorrow for my official statement, and maybe that will bring a little joy to you too."

"It will. It does. I appreciate what you've done." She waved to him as she climbed into her car.

Cheryl listened to Christmas carols and sang along to her favorites on her drive home. Of course, there was no guarantee that what Mr. Chetty had done would make any difference, but the fact that he'd taken his time to clear things up concerning Levi meant a lot.

Seth and Naomi had again come to stay with the kids, and Cheryl expected them to be quite worn out after the last few days of doing the same. Yet when she opened the door, there was a rush of colors and scents within her home.

She took in a breath, taking in the aroma of pine, chocolate, and yeasty bread. A squeal sounded from the living room, and two blurs raced toward her. Cheryl quickly slipped off her coat.

With giggles and exclamations, Rebecca and Matthew jumped into her arms.

"Hey now. You're going to topple me over," she said, laughing. Her cheeks were still chilled from the brisk air outside, yet her children were sweaty and warm from running around inside. With a smile, she kissed the tops of their heads, and when she got a better look at the room, she saw that they'd been getting everything ready for Christmas.

Rebecca jumped up and down and pointed to the tree. "Opa took us out in the deep, deep snow, and we cut down the tree!

Then, Oma helped us bake. We made cinnamon rolls, and I smeared the white sugar icing all over the top!"

Naomi shuffled from the kitchen wearing Cheryl's apron and stirring something in a big bowl on her hip.

"Cheryl, I hope you do not mind." Naomi glanced up at her as she continued to whisk the spoon. "Seth and I are not as young as we used to be. We have found the best thing we can do to keep the children out of trouble is to keep them busy. I do not know what plans you had for a Christmas tree, but Seth took the children out and found one on your property. I think it turned out very well, don't you?"

Cheryl gazed at the delightful tree. From the looks of it, they had found one of the boxes of ornaments from the garage and hung them too, or at least the kids had hung them. Cheryl chuckled, seeing that all the decorations were on the lower half of the tree.

"Naomi, I don't mind at all. I was worried about getting a tree up for the kids. My mind has been busy with so many things." She took a step forward and placed an arm around Seth's shoulders before she remembered that displays of affection weren't the Amish way.

Cheryl laughed as he stood there awkwardly. Then she kissed him on the cheek for good measure. "Thank you, Seth. It's wonderful. It's perfect. I'm so thankful that you and the kids had a fun day. It's just like something Levi would do." Tears filled Cheryl's eyes as she said her husband's name.

"And did you get a chance to talk to Levi?" Naomi asked.

"No, because of some type of sickness, the prisoners are quarantined in their rooms. I hope he hasn't caught anything."

Cheryl bit her lower lip. "I'm sure if he was sick, they would have told me."

Concern filled Naomi's eyes, and Cheryl didn't want to disrupt the festive feel of the moment. "Naomi, those cinnamon rolls look so wonderful. I'm starving. Rebecca, could you put one on a plate for me?"

Rebecca flipped her curls behind her shoulder and crossed her arms over her chest. "Mama," she said with an exasperated sigh, "you're going to eat a cinnamon roll before dinner?"

Cheryl wondered how she should answer. She always told the kids that having sugar before dinner would ruin their appetite. But from the twinkle in Naomi's eyes, Cheryl knew that just this once, it would be okay. "Tell you what, let's all have cinnamon rolls for dinner. And then why don't we order pizza for dessert? Naomi, Seth, would you like to stay?"

"You know, I haven't had pizza in a while." Naomi sat with a plop into a chair. "And now that your maam is here, Rebecca, I think that's a *goot* idea. So I'm going to put my feet up and wait for that pizza to be delivered."

They enjoyed dinner and dessert together, and Seth and Naomi shared stories of what Levi was like as a child. Matthew loved to hear about his daddy as a little boy driving his pony cart to their one-room Amish school. Rebecca liked to hear that Levi would sneak small critters into the house as pets. The story she liked the best was one about a squirrel that didn't want to be a pet as much as Levi wanted it to be.

Naomi turned to Seth. "Do you remember waking up in the middle of the night to hear Sarah screaming? She heard something going on in Levi's room, so she went to tell him to be quiet. And as soon as she opened the door, that squirrel ran out right between her legs. Sarah never cared much for squirrels after that."

Seth's laughter rumbled through the room. "Ja, and I think that is how she got her nickname, Sarah Squirrel. Didn't her brothers call her that for a few years?"

"Indeed they did." Naomi chuckled. As their merriment faded, her eyes took on a faraway gaze. She sighed. "Although those children kept us busy, it was a goot, goot time. Right, Seth?"

"Ja, Wife. Those were goot times, and these are goot times still." He glanced at his grandchildren. "*Gott* has a good way of caring for us. I am trusting that this Christmas even more of His wonderful care will be revealed. We simply have to open our hearts to Him, even in the midst of troubles. Would you agree?"

Cheryl nodded. "That's exactly what He's teaching me too. As each day nears Christmas, I'm eager to see what gifts our good God will bring."

CHAPTER NINETEEN

heryl's cell phone buzzed bright and early. She glanced at the clock and jumped. "Who in the world would be calling me at seven in the morning?" she mumbled. She looked at the number, and it wasn't one she recognized. Cheryl rubbed the sleep from her eyes and answered it. "Hello?"

"Cheryl? Good morning. Did I wake you?"

Cheryl sat up straight. She brushed the tangle of hair from her face. "Levi, you're calling me. Why? Is everything all right? You're not sick, are you?"

Levi chuckled. "Slow down, slow down, give me a chance to speak. I am not sick. In fact, I am one of the few who are fine. They have me in a separate area, and the police officer here today is nice. She said I could call. Can you believe that, Cheryl? She is letting me use the phone."

"Can you tell her thank you for me?" Cheryl put her pillow behind her back and leaned against the headboard. She could hear him talking to the woman, but she couldn't make out the words. Then he was back on the phone.

"Officer Sutton said that you were nice to her yesterday, and it was the least that she could do."

Cheryl was so thankful to finally hear Levi's voice on the other end of the phone. "Oh, Levi. It's so good to talk to you. I'm so glad you're not sick."

"Yes, thankfully, I have not gotten sick. I think I will be okay." Words poured out of Levi, probably because he didn't know how long he could be on the phone. "I should ask you the same thing. I guess that you have been running around town trying to get answers, while also taking care of the kids. How are they? How are you?"

"Good, good," Cheryl said quickly. "Your parents have been helping so much, and your sisters, and Judith." She too felt pressed for time. "But there are some things I need to ask you. And I need to apologize."

"What do you mean?"

"Well, I want to apologize for not listening better. I remember you talking about the tree limbs and the issues they were causing for the creek. But I didn't understand that there was a claim against us that you were trying to deal with. Levi, I'm so sorry that you had to carry that burden alone." She sighed and tucked a wayward curl behind her ear. "You tried to tell me so many times. But I didn't listen very well. I was too easily distracted—"

"Or you fell asleep." He laughed.

"Yes, thank you for bringing that up." She laughed too.

"Well, it was easy to let it go because I didn't want to worry you." Levi cleared his throat. "Although sometimes we are not in the right, even if we are doing the right thing."

"What do you mean?"

"Ohio law makes it clear that property lines extend to the sky. I visited Rudy's place numerous times. I talked to Rudy's wife, telling her of my plans. I even left a note for him—twice—but Rudy never got back to me. I feel terrible because even though I was in the right, I hurt Rudy's business deal."

"Levi, I was so excited to hear your voice that I almost forgot to tell you. I don't think you ruined his business deal after all."

"What do you mean?"

"I talked to Rich Chetty from Sugarcreek Realty. The story is too long to go into, but he admitted that he received an email from Rudy saying that he was taking the house off the market, and it was before you cut down those limbs. He said he even called Chief Twitchell yesterday and told him that."

Levi was quiet, and Cheryl heard the softest sniffle. Then he cleared his throat again. "Listen, I need to go, but it was so good to hear your voice. And can you make sure Maam knows that I am okay? She tends to worry."

"Yes, of course. I'll let your mom know. Oh, I wish the kids were awake—"

"Next time," Levi said in a rush. "I have to go. I love you, Cheryl."

The call ended, and Cheryl pressed her phone to her heart, so thankful for his call. She hadn't done a very good job of listening to Levi before, but that was going to change. After getting the kids up and dressed for breakfast, she would head over to her in-laws' place and let Naomi know that Levi was doing well.

An hour later, she had two kids bundled and excited to be going to Oma and Opa's house. Elizabeth greeted them in the driveway and invited the kids to head to the barn with her. Rebecca and Matthew jumped out of the car excitedly and joined her. They were always excited about things to see and do with their aunt.

Cheryl hurried up the front porch steps, her heart still filled from hearing Levi's voice. She opened the front door, and the delicious smells of baking hit her. Two older women worked alongside Naomi, and Cheryl smiled to see Levi's aunts.

"It looks like everyone's in the mood for baking Christmas cookies." Cheryl took off her coat, walked up to a tray, and stole a gingersnap. "Don't worry about me. I'm happy to be your taste-tester." She took a bite and sighed with pleasure, bringing happy laughter from Levi's aunts.

Naomi washed her hands, wiped them on a dishtowel, and then walked over to Cheryl. "How is everything?" Her eyes searched Cheryl's face. "Do you have good news? There seems to be a brightness in your eyes today."

"Yes, I got to talk to Levi. He's doing very well. He's not sick, and one of the police officers let him call home. I'm not sure if anything is going to change with the charges against him, but just hearing his voice gave me so much hope. God is holding up both of us."

"It is good to see your smile, and why don't we keep up the merry spirit? You said the other day that you have not had a chance to wrap presents or do the shopping you wanted. Why don't you leave the children here and see how much you can get done?"

"Oh, I don't want to do that to you. It looks like you're busy. It's not every day your sisters are here."

"Nonsense. Elizabeth just took the children to the barn, and the kittens are so adorable. We will not see them for hours."

"If you're sure, I'll run back home and get some things done, and then I'll come back this evening. Will that work?"

"Yes, yes." Naomi waved her away. "Christmas is coming, Cheryl, and I have a feeling we're going to celebrate."

The gusty wind pushed Cheryl from store to store, but the bright sunshine made it feel not so cold. She usually fretted over what to buy for her family, but she didn't this year. She didn't have time. So instead, she scanned each store to see what caught her eye. A new doll for Rebecca with hand-sewn clothes. For Matthew, a soft robe with large elephant ears on the hood and a cuddly stuffed elephant to match. A ceramic teacup with a wooden handle for Naomi, a tea strainer, and a few tea choices. And for Levi a new work jacket that wasn't torn and stained—and one that she'd be able to wear to town if she needed to.

Happy with those and other purchases, Cheryl had barely hung her coat on the rack at home when there was a knock at the door. Through the door's window, she could see a black bonnet over a white kapp. With a smile, Cheryl opened the door and waved Naomi inside.

Naomi bustled in. She carried a basket with a cloth over it. All sorts of warm smells of baked goods rose from the basket.

"My sister was passing this direction, and I asked for a ride. Seth will be by later with the children, but I had a nudge that I needed to come now."

"Naomi, we still have all the food you made from the other day. I'm going to gain twenty pounds just trying to keep up with it all."

"Well, I was thinking about Rudy's wife. What is her name? Astrid?"

Cheryl thought for a moment. She had spoken to Rudy's wife at least a half-dozen times, but for as long as they'd lived next door, that wasn't much. "Let me think. Rudy, Owen, yes, Astrid. That's it."

Naomi nodded. "It must be so hard for her to have her husband in the hospital at such a time as this. I thought we should take her some treats and a couple of loaves of bread. I made soup too. We should go check on her. Homemade food makes everything better." She set the basket on the table and then placed her hands on her hips and squared her shoulders. "The food I make is not very grand, but it is great."

Laughter spilled from Cheryl's lips. "Did you just come up with that?"

"My oma did, but I have taken it as my own."

Cheryl glanced at the basket of food, and then she imagined going over to Astrid's house and knocking on the door. She took a step back and slowly eased herself onto one of the kitchen chairs. She felt the smile fall from her face. "I don't know if I can do this."

"Why not?"

"What if Astrid is upset with me? What if she's angry with Levi? What if she thinks that he really did something to hurt her husband? It could bring more conflict."

Naomi sighed. "I think that is some of the trouble we have these days. We tend to worry too much. We come up with all sorts of problems. Our minds are always looking for ways to keep us safe, but we often forget that kindness usually smooths things over.

The worst-case scenario is we get there and Astrid slams the door on us. The best case, Astrid will receive a little kindness—when she needs it most. And you will have a bit more peace too." Naomi picked up the basket. "Finally, in the middle of 'he said this' and 'he did that,' maybe the two of you will be able to talk."

Cheryl looked out the window. The sky was clear blue. The sun reflected off the snow. It was a beautiful day for a walk, especially for a walk down the lane and over to the neighbor's house. She could sit here and think of all the ways to help her husband, or she could go with Naomi and take this basket to Astrid.

Cheryl thought of Levi. She did not doubt what he would do. Levi was always one to give kindness. He would want to talk to Astrid. He would have already been over there to check on her and see how she was doing. He would be over there helping Astrid with her chores, no matter what anyone said about him.

"You know, my aunt Mitzi said something that I needed to hear." Cheryl stood. "She wrote a letter to me and said, 'It's always the right time to do the right thing.' For a while now, I've been meaning to reach out to Astrid. More than once, Rebecca has asked if we could take cookies over to her. Early in the summer, Astrid brought over some things from her garden. She was so kind to share what she had. I've been meaning to do something to thank her. And now, this might be it. Yes, I think walking down there is exactly what I want to do today."

Chapter Twenty

It didn't take more than ten minutes for Cheryl and Naomi to tromp down the Miller driveway in their boots and then walk a short way down the road and up the Wight driveway. If it hadn't been for Naomi pointing it out, Cheryl wouldn't have noticed the trees that had shorter branches on one side over the fence line. They weren't wholly sheared off at the base of the trunk like she'd assumed.

Cheryl eyed the trees as she walked. She carried the large basket filled with wonderful things, her arms wrapped around it in front of her, and the scents met her nose with each step. "I bet in spring new leaves will cover those branches and it'll hardly be noticeable."

Naomi paused as they got closer. "Actually, for this type of maple, they do well with shaping. In the late spring, the same can be done on the side over the Wight road and it will create straight, tall columns. Oh, can you imagine how beautiful that will look next fall when these trees change into dazzling colors?"

Cheryl eyed Naomi. "How on earth do you know that?"

"My uncle used to work for a tree-trimming service." She chuckled and continued, her boots crunching on the snow. "He was a talker, that one. He would go on and on about all types of trees and how to best care for them. If you put me in a tree trivia game, I would win every time."

"So if Levi volunteered to come and trim the other side of the trees, that would help balance everything out?"

"Yes, and it would be beautiful, just beautiful. And if he added a layer of mulch at the base to keep in moisture, these trees will be drawing visitors from miles around. You know, pruning is a good thing for maple trees. It helps them maintain optimal health."

Cheryl grinned. "Oh, I can't wait to tell him. I'll have him be the one to talk to Rudy about it. It'll be good news for their relationship."

A lightness filled Cheryl's heart, and she fancied she'd be able to float if not for the heavy layers of clothes she was wearing.

"I do love how you are talking about Rudy waking up, and he and Levi reconciling. I have been praying for Rudy—as I know you have. Faith changes things, doesn't it? Not only for the people we are praying for but for us too."

"Yes, I agree." Cheryl's stride slowed as they neared the Wight house and walked up the porch steps. The sound of a dog barking greeted them as they stood on the covered front porch. It wasn't the sound of a farm dog. Instead, it was the small yips of a tiny dog.

Cheryl smiled, thinking of what Levi would say. "*There's no use for a purse dog on a farm.*" But then again, a purse dog could keep someone company during a tough time, so there was a good use for that type of dog in any home.

Naomi knocked, and thirty seconds later the door swung open. Astrid's eyes widened. For a moment, fear flickered within their gray depths. The heavy screen door slipped in her hand, and Cheryl thought the woman was going to slam it in their faces until she caught it and opened it wider. Astrid looked from Cheryl's face to Naomi's, to the basket, and then to Cheryl's face again. "Cheryl, I didn't expect you. Would you like to come in?"

The woman had to be in her midforties with short-cropped brown hair and a flawless complexion. Today she had dark circles under her eyes, and Cheryl could see she'd been crying. Astrid slowly stepped back and beckoned them inside. Even then, her movements looked unsure. Cheryl knew why once she glanced down and saw the unwieldy medical boot that reached almost to Astrid's knee.

She offered as broad a smile as she could manage with the trembling in her stomach. "Astrid, yes. We would love to come in. This is my mother-in-law, Naomi. I don't know if you've met her before."

Together they stepped inside, and Astrid shut the door behind them. The room was colder than Cheryl had expected. A woodstove in the corner seemed to give off very little heat. A pile of dishes sat on the counter by the kitchen sink. But the rest of the room was tidy with everything in its place, including the shiny, black-handled kettle and ceramic jars lined up in a row.

Other than the yipping dog, the only other sound was the fridge motor rumbling. But once the dog saw that they were not dangerous, he promptly climbed back into his doggy bed near the kitchen table and lowered his head on his paws to watch.

"I'm so sorry this place looks such a mess. I've been at the hospital." Astrid stopped short, and tears filled her eyes as she looked down at her feet as if suddenly the most fascinating thing in the world sat right there in front of her toes. "Please have a seat."

Cheryl set the basket on the table. The basket weighed nothing compared to her heavy heart. She was happy to sit. Just being here seemed to seep all the energy from her. She had been grieving for Levi, but he was still healthy, even though he was sitting inside a jail cell. Rudy, on the other hand, was lying unconscious in a hospital bed. Naomi sat in the chair next to Cheryl and took her hand, infusing strength into her.

"How is Rudy?" Cheryl asked.

Tears filled Astrid's eyes. She unfolded a towel on the counter and used it to dab the tears that spilled down her cheeks. "He is stable. We can be thankful for that. Owen is sitting up there with him now. He told me to come home and try to get some rest, but it's so hard, you know?"

"I'm so glad Owen's there. It's difficult spending long days at the hospital." Cheryl patted the basket. "We brought some soup and bread. There are some Christmas cookies in here that my kids helped decorate too." She smiled. "Don't mind the fingerprints."

"Owen will especially love those, and I promise he'll eat every one. I haven't baked for him this year...." Her voice trailed off.

"My husband, Seth, and I have been praying for your husband," Naomi said. "Do they say what the prognosis is?"

"Rudy had a bad head injury, and he has a broken collarbone and fractured arm. They had to operate a few times, but now everything is set, and it looks like the pressure was relieved on his brain. They're giving him medication to keep him in a coma so he will rest for a while. They tell me that they need to do that so his brain has time to heal."

Weeks of hospital stays—not days—stretched ahead of him, Cheryl guessed. She glanced at the shopping list on the fridge and made a mental note of the items to pick up the next time she was at the store. She needed to do more for Astrid, and she'd talk to Naomi about reaching out to others in the community to help too.

Compassion filled Cheryl's heart. "It was such a horrible thing. Such a severe accident at what was supposed to be a special occasion. I've also been praying for Rudy. And I'll continue to pray for you too, Astrid."

Astrid moved to sit in the chair opposite Cheryl. "Thank you," she said.

An awkward silence filled the room. Cheryl noticed a family photo hanging on the wall in the hallway that led into the kitchen. In the photo, Rudy and Astrid looked much younger, both with brown hair that didn't show any hint of gray. And Owen, as a toddler, sat on their laps, beaming.

Cheryl cleared her throat. "I'm sure it's hard dealing with so much, especially around Christmas. Is Owen doing well?"

"He's trying to be a help. I don't know how well you know Owen, but he has special needs. Thankfully, he's able to drive. It's helpful that he can go sit with his father, but he can only stay so long. The hospital is an overwhelming place for Owen to be." Astrid again wiped a few tears away and twisted her wedding ring around her finger. "The truth is, I have no desire to celebrate at all. Rudy and I were married when I was eighteen, and he was

184 | Sugarcreek Amish Mysteries

twenty-three. I've had far more Christmases with him than without. Rudy's the one who always made the holidays—and life—a celebration. He was the one with the big dream to have this property. I don't know what I'd do with it if he wasn't around. There's just so much to manage. We sold all of our animals when we planned on selling this place, and I'm glad now. The only one I have to care for is Coco here, and I can do that. Owen is nearly twenty, and he pretty much takes care of his own needs, but I can't imagine that he'll be able to live on his own anytime soon."

Which makes it unlikely that Owen would plot to harm his father and take over the property, Cheryl thought. She rubbed her hands together. "And do you have enough wood for the woodstove?"

"Oh yes. I just need to have Owen bring some in. I keep forgetting." Astrid pointed to the medical boot on her foot. "I did this a couple of weeks ago. I stepped off the front porch the wrong way. I've been trying to stay home and take it easy. That's why I wasn't there for the opening of the nativity. But deep down, I'm glad I wasn't. I don't know if I could have handled it. To see Rudy fall like that. It was bad enough hearing Owen talk about it."

"I hope you know how sorry I am that he was hurt. I know Levi is sorry too. He asked about how Rudy is doing. I hope you don't mind that I told him that Rudy is stable but that we also need to keep praying for a complete recovery."

Astrid nodded. "I'm not surprised he asked. Levi is such a nice man. I know the police have arrested him, but I told them Levi didn't do this." Her voice trembled as she said the last words, but the conviction in her tone surprised Cheryl.

"But have the police kept you up-to-date on what they found?"

"Oh yes. I know it was not an accident. They didn't listen when I told them Levi wasn't involved, but since I can't give them more to go on, they have no other choice."

Cheryl glanced at Naomi, who lifted her eyebrows in curiosity. Did she notice the mix of anger and fear in the woman's tone too? It was clear that Astrid believed Levi was innocent. However, more challenging was telling if she believed that someone else might be guilty—somebody she knew.

Even though Cheryl told herself to let it drop and just to enjoy this visit, she couldn't. "The way this happened wasn't an accident. Did Rudy have any enemies? Do you know of anyone who would want to hurt him?"

Astrid's eyebrows furrowed slightly, and the briefest spark of anger flashed in her eyes. If Cheryl hadn't been looking at her, she would have missed it.

Does she know? Is Astrid keeping the name of the person who did this from the police?

"Oh, well, Rudy is a very stubborn man. When he's upset, everyone knows about it." Astrid swept her arms and shrugged as if saying that her guess was as good as anyone else's. Then she chuckled softly to herself. "Rudy's stubborn when it comes to this house and property too. He has a lot of big ideas. He had a lot of plans for this farm until it was clear they would be impossible to act on."

Cheryl was certain Astrid had more to say, and so she sat quietly. It was a trick she'd learned from Naomi. Often the best way to get answers wasn't to rush in with question after question but instead to sit back and remain still until the person grew nervous with the silence and kept talking.

"Rudy has never been one to mince words," Astrid continued after a long pause. "But that doesn't mean he's unreasonable. I wasn't at the church the other day, but I did hear that Rudy had words with Levi." Astrid reached down to the dog bed and lifted her little dog onto her lap. "He's like Coco—a lot of bark but no bite."

"Do you know of Rudy and Levi having words like that, fighting, any other time?" Naomi asked.

"I can't say that I do." Astrid paused and looked up at the ceiling. She squinted as if replaying different scenes in her mind, checking for accuracy. "But honestly, I never remember Rudy and Levi having a chance to talk. Levi came by several times, and he told me that he wanted to talk to Rudy. I think he left a note too, at least once. I would always tell my husband, but there have been some family issues that he's been trying to help out with. He said he would get back to Levi. He promised he would. But I doubt he ever did."

"Did Rudy ever say anything to suggest that he was suing us? That he was mad at Levi?"

"No. And I was shocked to hear that Levi was arrested. There were others, well, I don't know how to say this. There are others that I would have been less surprised to hear..." Astrid let her words trail off.

"Wait, what do you mean?" Naomi asked. "You just said that Rudy didn't have any enemies, didn't you?"

"Rudy didn't have any *enemies*, but there were many people interested in this property. Not Owen. I want to make that clear. There were family members who thought they deserved to profit from a sale, but Rudy wasn't about to sell our place to just anyone. He loves his land, and he wanted to make sure it went to someone who would take care of it. Who would maintain its beauty."

Cheryl leaned closer. "Are you saying there are family members who wanted Rudy to sell?"

"Well, *a* family member, but that's saying too much. I shouldn't really be talking to anyone about this without Rudy here. That's why I haven't said anything to the police. Rudy said that family problems need to stay in the family. He said I didn't need to worry about it, that he'd take care of everything. Rudy didn't like to see me worked up."

The more Astrid spoke, the more her knee bounced, and Cheryl could almost imagine Astrid's heartbeat quickening within her chest. "Not that Rudy would have ever considered anyone in his family an enemy," she continued. "He tried to go along with this person's idea, but he could only go so far. When the buyer wanted to put in a large subdivision, Rudy couldn't go through with it. He said he'd rather have a relative mad at him than to see his land broken up into pieces and covered with houses and roads. He sent an email to the Realtor and stopped the deal. Am I making any sense?" Even though she said the words, Astrid didn't speak with confidence. And instead of making eye contact, she looked at the dog on her lap, petting him briskly.

Cheryl leaned back in her chair, eyeing the woman. Something had gotten her agitated. Astrid had been fine talking about Levi. She had been fine talking about Rudy and his injuries. But as soon as Cheryl started asking about who else might want to hurt Rudy, anxiety showed up in every crease of Astrid's face and her body movements. It was clear that she believed a family member was involved. Even the dog seemed bothered by it. He jumped from his owner's lap and curled back up in his bed.

"It's so nice of you to bring these baked goods," Astrid finally said, rising. "The soup smells wonderful too, thank you."

Cheryl took that as a sign that it was time for them to go, yet she knew she'd regret it if she didn't ask one more thing. So she stood and turned to her neighbor. "I promise I didn't come over here to ask questions, but since we're on the topic, can you tell me if you think this family member was the one who hurt Rudy?"

"I don't want to think so." She jutted out her chin. "I don't know this person well," she said as she ushered them out. "And that's another reason why I can't say anything. I'm here alone, you know. I'm sure you understand, Cheryl, how hard it is to be alone and have the one who cares for you unable to be here, unable to help."

Cheryl did know. And she didn't blame Astrid for being cautious. She didn't blame her at all.

CHAPTER TWENTY-ONE

I t felt good to have a happy day. Well, as happy as a day could be without Levi at home. In the afternoon, when Seth brought the children home, the sun was bright in the sky and snow melted from the roof and dripped off the eaves.

Seth and the kids had just returned from the barn after doing chores, and Cheryl heard them cleaning up in the bathroom. She smiled, guessing that Rebecca and Matthew would rope Opa into giving them horsey rides on his knee or reading them stories. Thankfully, Seth was usually accommodating.

Cheryl stared out the window, her eyes moving beyond their farm to the one next door. She turned to Naomi, who was emptying the dish drainer. "You know, I've been thinking. It was nice that we took one meal over, but I'm sure Astrid could benefit from more."

"Ja, I think you are right about that," Naomi said. "I will talk to some of our neighbors, and we will provide meals while Rudy is laid up." She put the last fork in the silverware drawer and pushed it closed. "We can even get some of the men to help her out with the heavier chores. Even though they have sold their animals, that does not mean there is not work she might need help with."

Cheryl returned to peering out the window and saw the now familiar white truck parked on the road again.

"There is also something very strange, Naomi. Do you see that truck out there? There's a young woman who has been taking photos, a lot of photos, of Rudy's property."

"Just Rudy's property?"

"Well, sometimes I catch her taking photos of our place too."

Naomi moved to the window to look. "That is interesting. Have you seen this happening often?"

"Just in the last three or four days. Sometimes I wonder if she read about Levi being arrested in the newspaper. What if she's one of those true-crime podcasters who's trying to find more information about this case? Or maybe she's with the newspaper, and she's watching us, waiting to see what our next move is." Cheryl's shoulders tightened. She couldn't imagine living like this all the time. She stepped back from the window and turned to see a large smile on Naomi's face.

Cheryl's jaw dropped open in surprise. "Do you think this is funny?"

"Well, maybe if I knew what a podcast was."

"A podcast is like a radio show, but it's streamed over the internet, and anyone from anywhere in the world can listen in." Cheryl smiled then too, knowing that her explanation wasn't helping anything. All of those words were unfamiliar to her Amish mother-in-law.

"I see." Naomi tilted her head and stroked her chin. "Cheryl, do you really think that woman is from a true-crime podcast? This is Sugarcreek. Folks around here just need to talk to their neighbors to figure out what's going on. And why would anyone beyond our community be interested in two feuding neighbors?"

"That's precisely it." Cheryl pointed her finger into the air. "It's a small community. People love listening to that type of stuff. It's always the Friendly Farmer that no one suspects."

"Except this time."

"Yes, except this time."

Naomi shook her head. "I think you listen to the news too much. That is one thing—among many others—that I appreciate about not having a television or radio. Our minds do not get filled with someone else's ideas."

Cheryl spun away from the window. "I'm not going to just stand here and wonder." She went into her bedroom, to the closet, and found Levi's binoculars. Then she went back to the window and trained the lenses on the side of the pickup. "She shows up around the same time every day," she said to Naomi. "Four o'clock in the afternoon."

Cheryl watched, and after a couple of minutes, the young woman again got in her truck and drove away. But this time Cheryl had written down the company name and phone number printed on the cab.

As she put the binoculars down, Beau approached. He meowed, rubbing against her legs.

Naomi walked into the pantry and reemerged with Beau's food. "Hi there, Beau. I bet you are hungry." She picked up his bowl and shook some food into it.

Over the last week, Cheryl had gotten used to the extra help, but she knew she couldn't let Seth and Naomi interrupt their own lives for her much longer. Her body tensed at the thought that she'd have to figure out real life on her own soon, but she refused even to think what that real life could be like if it didn't include Levi. *No, I'm not going to think of that at all.*

Naomi made herself helpful doing other things, including tackling the laundry. Cheryl tried to sweep the floor, but she couldn't get her mind off the young woman. Finally, getting up the nerve, she dialed the number that she'd jotted down, but it went straight to voice mail.

"Thank you for calling LLC Construction and Remodel. We would love to help you turn your house into a home. Our business hours are Monday through Friday, nine a.m. to three p.m. Leave a message, and we'll be sure to call back."

Cheryl set her phone down with a sigh. If a construction company was involved, maybe a land developer had already put things into motion. Perhaps someone believed the property would be for sale soon now that Rudy was in the hospital. She didn't doubt that if things had been just a tiny bit worse with Rudy, that's probably what would have happened. After all, there was no way Astrid could take care of that place on her own.

After the kitchen floor was swept, Cheryl found Naomi in Rebecca's room, helping Rebecca fold and put away her laundry. Rebecca put a finger to her lips as Cheryl entered. "Quiet, Matthew is sleeping. Opa was rocking him in Matthew's bedroom, and both of them fell asleep."

Cheryl laughed. "Well, it's good to know they're getting some rest."

As soon as she finished putting her clothes away, Rebecca pulled her doll carriage out of her closet. "I'm going to go give

Beau a ride!" She ran out of the room with a giggle, dragging the stroller behind her.

"I'm sure Beau's going to love that!" Cheryl called after her daughter, shaking her head.

"Never a dull moment." Naomi sat down on Rebecca's bed with a sigh. "So, did you ever figure out that mysterious young woman? I saw you write down the number."

Cheryl sat beside her. "It's a company truck from a construction company. I have a feeling someone is counting on Rudy wanting to sell because of this ordeal. Maybe it's the same investor who was interested in the property before Rudy took it back off the market. Maybe they're already plotting the land for a subdivision and all the dozens of houses that they're going to put in."

"So you do not think it is a true-crime whatever-you-called-it anymore?"

Cheryl laughed. "No, probably not."

"Well, maybe you should call and ask the young woman what she is doing."

"I tried, but it went straight to voice mail."

"Did you leave a message?"

Cheryl paused. "Well, no."

"There is an Amish proverb that says, 'Beware of half-truths. You may have hold of the wrong half.'"

Cheryl laughed. "Or maybe I'm completely wrong."

"We come up with all sorts of ideas. And most of them are not true. How can they be true when there is only one truth?" Naomi stood. "So my suggestion is just to call, leave a message, and ask the young woman what she is doing. It does not seem like she is doing any harm. And even if she works for a land developer, there is no saying what will happen with the land. We are praying for Rudy's recovery, and no one can determine what is next."

Heat rose to Cheryl's cheeks. "I think you're right. The office won't be open until Monday. I'll think about what to say, and then I'll leave a message."

Naomi reached down and patted Cheryl's hand. "You have had a lot on your mind, and I imagine you have not been getting much rest. Seth and Matthew are napping, and I am happy to entertain Rebecca if you would like to go lie down."

"Really? You would do that?" Cheryl yawned. "I haven't had a good nap since both of the kids started moving and never seemed to slow down. And you're right. Lately I've been up half the night trying to think through everything I've learned. And sadly, I haven't gotten as many answers as I've hoped for."

Naomi moved to the living room to check on Rebecca, and Cheryl walked to her bedroom and climbed into her unmade bed. It felt strange to get into bed when the sun was still bright outside, yet comfortable too. She heard Christmas music playing in the living room, and Cheryl assumed that Rebecca had talked Naomi into turning on the radio, maybe while they baked or made a craft.

Cheryl tucked the pillow under her chin and finally faced the fact that Christmas was just three days away. Knowing that Levi would most likely not be with them this year caused a familiar ache. Many years ago, she had felt the same way when she was sure she would never have a family to celebrate Christmas with or a home to do it in.

For many months after breaking up with her fiancé, Lance, Cheryl believed the worst thing in the world had to be spending the holidays alone. She had awakened Christmas morning without someone there to celebrate with. She had stayed up on New Year's Eve with a list of dreams, not even daring to hope they'd come true. Things had seemed so hopeless back then, but the highs and lows she was facing now might be worse.

Yes, it had to be worse having such close companionship with Levi and then losing it. Cheryl tried not to be too dramatic. She hadn't lost Levi. But her bed was lonely and cold without him, even with bright sunlight streaming in.

Cheryl closed her eyes. She rubbed her feet together under the flannel sheets, trying to get them warm. She remembered when she first got to know Levi as that Amish man who leaned against her counter at the Swiss Miss and regarded her with sparkling blue eyes that matched his button-down shirt. It had surprised her how his rugged handsomeness had drawn her heart right from the beginning. She laughed softly to herself, realizing how handsome she still thought he was now, especially when he walked in with his sleeves rolled up from a day of work on their family farm. Their farm. Their family.

Dear Lord, thank You for Levi. I thank You that You are with him now. I pray that You will provide him with peace, even as Christmas nears. I thank You that You are with Chief Twitchell and Carlos. I pray that You will lead them to the answers, since I don't see very many myself. I also thank You that You are with Rudy, and I pray for his healing.

Lord, I pray that whatever conflict has been between our family and our neighbors, You will use it to bring us closer together. Thank You for being with me. I thank You, Lord, that I never have to be alone.

CHAPTER TWENTY-TWO

Cheryl had napped longer than she'd expected, and all the light outside had faded. She glanced at the clock and saw that it was almost six. Naomi was right. She had needed the rest. And thankfully, she woke with sweet peace, being reminded again that God was with her and Levi both.

The house was strangely quiet as she walked into her kitchen. She scanned the room, wondering if Naomi and Seth had taken the kids to their house. Then Cheryl heard soft talking. She walked to the living room and saw Seth, Naomi, and her children sitting on the floor. There was a box opened in front of them, and old photos were spread around them. Cheryl recognized the images immediately. Church pageants, a small-town parade. Cheryl, around age six, with her dad at the local mercantile store.

"What do you have there?"

Four sets of eyes turned in her direction. Naomi looked as if she'd just been caught with her hand in the cookie jar, and Cheryl immediately knew why. The Amish, including her in-laws, did not pose for photographs, considering it a violation of the second commandment, which prohibited the capturing of graven images. Although Naomi pretended that she didn't notice when Cheryl took out her phone to snap a photo of her children with their grandparents, the older woman would not allow Cheryl to take her picture by herself, believing it promoted individualism and vanity. And yet here they were, looking through old photographs, mainly from Cheryl's childhood.

Cheryl appreciated how her in-laws had softened over time. They no longer stuck to their strict ideas as rigidly as they used to. These were memories that deserved to be captured.

"Oh Cheryl, I hope you do not mind. We were looking for the extra Christmas decorations you were telling us about, and we came across this old box of photos. Look at this." Naomi held up Cheryl's school picture from when she was in kindergarten. "I cannot believe how much you look like Rebecca, or rather how much Rebecca looks like you."

Cheryl moved to the couch to sit close to them. "Well, except for her bright blue eyes. Those are one hundred percent Levi." She accepted the photo from Naomi's hand and softly brushed her six-year-old face with the pad of her thumb. "Yes, I do recognize my wild red hair and full cheeks in my little girl." Cheryl reached over and softly pinched Rebecca's cheek.

Then she picked up another photo of her mom one Christmas morning. How long since she'd had a long talk with her parents? It had been two weeks at least. Lately the most she'd done was call to give them a quick update on Levi. She'd been so busy trying to fix the problem and find the answers herself that she'd missed out on the support her parents could offer, even from afar.

In the next photo, her mother sat on the floor in front of a thin pine tree covered in tinsel with a toddler no more than three years old sitting on her lap.

"And look." Naomi pointed to Cheryl's mother's smile. "There is Rebecca's grin too."

Cheryl's heart warmed as she gazed at the image of her mother. "I can't remember what made her laugh. Or what was in that box she just unwrapped. It was probably slippers. I'm not sure a year went by when my mother didn't receive a pair. But, yes, that's me sitting on her lap." Tears moistened Cheryl's eyes, and she quickly blinked them away.

She looked through more photos they had laid out, and she noticed that many of them were ones from Christmas. They stirred something in Cheryl. Even though those moments had passed decades ago, the feelings that warmed her inside were still there. The love those moments deposited in her remained. Cheryl placed a hand over her heart. She looked to Naomi, and her lower lip trembled.

"Ach, I am so sorry. I did not mean to upset you." Naomi's voice was soft.

"Oh no," Cheryl assured her. "It's not that at all. These are happy tears. They are good memories." She scanned the faces of her children. "It's yet another reminder of all I have to be thankful for—who I have to be grateful for—even during challenging circumstances."

"Look at this." Seth handed her another photo, releasing a deep chuckle with it. The picture showed an older Cheryl covered in tinsel, grinning and missing all four teeth in front. "You had such joy back then, ja?"

"Yes, I did. And I don't remember who hung that tinsel around my neck, but my mother was finding it around the house for days."

"Can we get some of that, Mama? I want to look pretty too," Rebecca chimed in.

Cheryl closed her eyes and winced. For a second, she tried to decide whether she wanted those sparkly threads scattered around her whole house. But then again, Rebecca wouldn't be six forever.

"Yes, I think we can work that out. We'll have to see if the stores have any."

"If not, I reckon you can order it on the internet," Seth piped up with a wink, as if ordering on the internet was the most natural thing in the world to him.

Belly laughter erupted from Cheryl at the thought of her father-in-law scrolling through items and shopping online.

"It's amazing how the love goes on and on in old photos, isn't it?" Cheryl regretted the words as soon as they were out of her mouth. She glanced at Naomi. "I'm so sorry."

"Oh, nothing to be sorry about." Naomi patted her temple. "I suppose that is what keeps our minds sharp in our old age. Having to store all those old memories up here." She sighed. "I do remember that first Christmas with Levi, Caleb, and Sarah. I was only twenty, as you may remember, and a new stepmother to three children. They had such fun, teaching me all about the traditions they had as a family around Christmastime. We baked and sang and told stories, and you never saw such escapades as we got into in the snow." Her eyes took on a faraway look. "Sarah, of course, was too little to remember that first Christmas we had together."

"Speaking of Sarah…" Cheryl's gaze moved from Naomi to Seth, knowing she probably shouldn't tell them what she was about to say. "I feel bad that I didn't tell you sooner, but Sarah and Joe are moving back to the area. They are currently looking for property."

Seth nodded, and although Cheryl almost expected his gaze to harden at the mention of his oldest daughter, it didn't. Instead, he reached forward and gently pulled one of Rebecca's curls. "I understand why you might have thought it would not be good to mention it. There have been seasons when things have been hard for me and her." He shrugged. "But I hope this is a new season."

"Where did you see Sarah?" Naomi's eyes were full of hope.

"Well, it's a long story, but first at the nativity event. Sarah and Joe left and actually didn't see the accident. And then I called and invited her over. She came the other day and spent time with me and the kids."

"Pay-doh, pay-doh!" Matthew shouted, running to his room to retrieve his gift.

"Yes, Auntie Sarah brought Play-Doh for the kids, and I was hoping we could invite her over for Christmas. Do you mind if we gather here? I think the kids and I will need that, in case…" Cheryl's voice trailed off. Everyone could guess what she was going to say. *In case Levi isn't home.*

"It will be good to have Sarah here," Naomi said. "We have a lot of catching up to do."

As they talked, Matthew ran to the kitchen table with his Play-Doh. Rebecca soon joined him, and they used cookie cutters to make their own Christmas cookies. Rebecca even broke off tiny bits of the modeling clay to make sprinkles to decorate the tops.

While Cheryl had been sleeping, Naomi lit candles in the living room and kitchen. Watching the kids make Play-Doh cookies in the candlelight was a beautiful scene. Naomi looked at Cheryl and tapped her temple again as if saying, "Yes, I am storing up this memory."

At the same time, Cheryl snapped photos on her phone. Far too soon, these moments would be gone. But more than that, she needed to capture them to share with Levi when he came home. She knew it would make him happy to know that there had been moments when the fear and worry had been pushed aside so they could take the time to celebrate the ordinary moments together.

"I'll call Sarah tomorrow and tell her that we'd love to have her and Joe for Christmas." Cheryl rose and moved to the fridge to discover what Naomi had made for dinner.

"Yes, well, I know that Esther and Elizabeth will be especially excited about that too. Elizabeth and Sarah always had a special bond. But for now, we must get home. Seth still has to finish up chores there, and I have a final bit of Christmas baking to do."

Cheryl walked them to the door and thanked them again. Then she ate a sandwich made from Naomi's thick, homemade bread. Soon it would be time for baths and bed.

It took longer to get the kids down for bed than usual. Cheryl tried all the tricks. She made hot cocoa. She read at least a dozen bedtime stories. And then she realized that the only way they would fall asleep was if Matthew was allowed to sleep in bed with Rebecca and if Cheryl stayed in the room until they fell asleep.

Everyone felt out of sorts with Levi gone. The kids said often how much they missed him too. Their daddy was their safety. He was their security. It didn't feel right when he was not home.

Cheryl must have drifted off to sleep in the beanbag chair in Rebecca's room. It was the chime of a Skype call that woke her with a start. Not so gracefully, she climbed out of the chair and rushed from the room before the ringing woke the kids. She hurried to her bedroom, flipped on the light, and answered the call. Her eyes were still adjusting when Aunt Mitzi's blurry face showed up on the screen.

It was so good to see her. The noonday sun was bright. Aunt Mitzi's face was tanned, and her hair was wet and curly. Cheryl knew that she had most likely just come in from outside. Even though Papua New Guinea had a hot, humid tropical climate all year round, December was the beginning of their wet season that would last until the end of March.

"Cheryl!" Aunt Mitzi's voice cracked. "I'm so sorry I didn't respond earlier. I just got home and saw your message. I was doing a Santa run through the jungles passing out gifts and sharing the good news of the real meaning of Christmas."

"Oh, Aunt Mitzi." As soon as the words got out of her mouth, Cheryl burst into tears. They blubbered out of her, and she sucked in big breaths to get them to stop.

"Oh, sweet girl. What's going on? You mentioned that Levi was accused of a crime that he didn't commit and that I needed to pray?"

Cheryl filled her aunt in on everything that had been happening. She first told Aunt Mitzi about the sabotaged nativity set and how Rudy Wight was critically hurt. Next, she shared how she'd initially thought that Owen and Joe had been involved, but she didn't believe that anymore.

"I also thought Rich Chetty from Sugarcreek Realty had a part in it, but again, I don't think that's the case." She shared about the young woman taking photos and about the lawsuit against Levi. It sounded like so much. Cheryl related how she'd searched every piece of evidence she'd run across and how little by little she'd uncovered the details surrounding their neighbor and his property. It was mind-boggling to share it all.

Compassion was evident in Aunt Mitzi's expression. "It sounds like you have been very busy, and in the middle of the holiday season too."

"Yes, well, God has sent all kinds of people to help me. Remember my friend Judith, who I've been calling my guardian angel? She's here for a visit. She's helped so much, and Seth and Naomi too."

"So a hard season has also been a season of blessings?" Aunt Mitzi's smile warmed Cheryl's heart even across the miles.

"It has been, and I've tried to be a blessing by giving to others. Judith and I blessed Mr. Chetty by decorating his office, and Naomi and I were able to take a meal to Rudy's wife, Astrid. Naomi's also working so that more families will be stepping up to help Astrid and Owen in the next few weeks."

Cheryl ran a hand through her messy hair. "You know, Aunt Mitzi, something you wrote in your last letter really helped me. You said, 'It's always the right time to do the right thing,' and I've really taken that to heart. When I felt completely overwhelmed, it was amazing how much it helped me to give."

"The Lord's ways aren't our ways, but when we make them our ways… Well, our way does go better!" Aunt Mitzi grinned. "Oh, and I forgot to ask. Did the package arrive with your presents?"

"Yes, and I have to ask you something. How did you know?"

"Know what?"

"Know that Sarah and Joe would be moving back to Sugarcreek. Know they'd be coming for Christmas. Know to send presents for them."

"They're moving back? That's wonderful news. I've known for a while that the Lord was going to bring some healing to that family. Sometimes the big conflicts that push us apart seem to shrink as the years pass. I'm eager to hear about the reconciliation that will soon be happening with the Millers. And as for how I knew?" Aunt Mitzi tapped her chin. "I'm not sure. It's just that when a thought pops into my mind that wasn't there a few minutes before, but it's something good to do, I just figure it's the Lord giving me direction."

Aunt Mitzi continued. "And speaking of direction, I want you to know that I've been praying for Levi even when I didn't know what was happening. As hard as this has been, the truth is that ultimately good will come out of it. Good for your family, and for your neighbors too. I trust that soon you'll be sending me the good news that Rudy is doing well and that Levi is home."

"Soon?" Cheryl perked up. "How soon?"

Aunt Mitzi shook her finger at the camera. "I wouldn't want to guess, and I suppose the 'when' isn't the most important part. God's timing is best whether it's tomorrow, next month, or next year. Unfortunately, I have to go, I've used up all my internet minutes, but Cheryl, I love you."

Aunt Mitzi's face disappeared, and Cheryl wished she could call her back and say goodbye. She knew it didn't matter though. Aunt Mitzi would still care and pray, pray and care. It felt good knowing she would, even on the other side of the world.

CHAPTER TWENTY-THREE

Knowing that she would be hosting Christmas at her house in two days put Cheryl into motion. Before heading into town, she had called Chief Twitchell. He'd been vague on the phone, but he told her he would be talking to Carlos, and he'd get back to her soon if they had any news. To keep her mind off waiting for the call, she'd taken the kids to buy groceries, and they searched through town to find tinsel. They finally found it at a small local grocery store chain, and when Cheryl saw the look on Rebecca's face, she marveled anew at how the smallest thing could mean so much to a child.

After shopping, Cheryl was pulling up to her driveway when she noticed the same young woman in the truck. She looked at her dashboard clock. Right around four o'clock. *What in the world is going on?*

Cheryl thought about what Naomi had said. To know the whole story, she just needed to ask. She parked by the woman's truck and got out. What would Naomi do? Naomi would be friendly and curious. Naomi wouldn't make any wrong assumptions. Naomi would probably invite the woman in for a cup of tea.

Of course, Cheryl didn't know if she'd go that far, but she could at least smile. The woman looked at Cheryl with a sheepish expression on her face. She started to put the lens cap on her camera, but Cheryl reached out a hand, waving it to tell her to stop. "I didn't mean to interrupt you. It looks like you're up to something important. I've just seen you out here a few times. I live on that farm right there." She pointed to her farm.

The woman nodded and smiled. "Yes, I've seen you before. You have a couple of kids, don't you?"

Cheryl laughed and pointed to the back seat of her car. "Yes, two kids, but sometimes it feels like they have as much energy as ten. They keep me busy, that's for sure."

The young woman released a breath. "I just love your farm. And the one next to it. They're so beautiful. And this time of day, the setting sun sends wonderful shadows over both of them. I've never seen such wonderful afternoon light as here in Ohio. I grew up in the South, and they don't have sunsets like this."

"And is that why you come at this time, because of the light?"

"Oh yes, I must have taken fifty photos of these fields by now." She held up her camera. "I'm trying to capture the perfect one and enter it into a photo contest. I'm a mom, and I help my husband with his construction company. I'm in the office with the kids until the afternoon, and by the time he gets off work, I can't wait to slip out for a few minutes and take some pictures. If I make the top ten in the contest, I'll get a complimentary conference registration. It's one of the best photo and video events in the country. I've wanted to go to it for a while."

Cheryl's eyes widened. "So you come here because of a photo contest? You're not part of a construction company that's interested in subdividing the land and putting in houses?"

"Oh no." The woman chuckled. Then she looked at the logo on the side of her truck, and understanding dawned on her face. "My husband is in construction, but we mainly remodel old houses. That's what he loves to do best anyway. Sometimes he'll build a garage or even help with a barn, but he's happiest when he's able to pull up the carpet in an old house and find wood floors underneath, and he can restore them good as new. You know, stuff like that."

"Well, I guess my imagination did run away with me, just like my mother-in-law said." But, of course, she'd be embarrassed to tell this young woman all the stories she'd made up in her mind.

The young woman looked back at the fields and the farms, and she released a sigh. "Out of all the farms in Sugarcreek, these are my favorite. There is so much peace here. It's almost as if you can step away from the conflict of the world for a time. I hope they never sell and subdivide these. That would be a horrible shame."

"I agree completely. I'm Cheryl, by the way."

"I'm Ari."

"If you have time, I can make us some tea. Although it might seem weird to be invited into a stranger's house."

"No, not weird at all. I've always wished that things could be that way. You know, like they used to be, where people in communities really got to know each other."

"Exactly, and I'm going to make a point to be that way more. To connect with the people around me. I feel as if most of my life is just running from one place to another with kids."

Ari took two steps toward her truck. "As much as I would like to, I need to get back and start dinner."

"Well, maybe next time," Cheryl said.

Ari slipped her camera into its case. "Yes, I would like that." She glanced at her watch and then walked the rest of the way back to her truck.

Cheryl moved to get into her car. "Oh, and Ari, I would love to see some of your photos sometime."

"Sure, of course."

"And I will send up a prayer tonight that one of yours will get picked. And that you would be able to go to that conference after all."

"I'm so glad you stopped, Cheryl. I got so worried every time I saw you. I didn't know if it was illegal or not to photograph someone's personal property. So I guess I should ask, do I have your permission?"

Cheryl gave her a thumbs-up. "Yes, you do, and the next time I talk to my neighbor, I'll make sure it's all right with her too."

Ari beamed. "Thank you. That means a lot. And maybe next time, I'll order pizza for my kids so I can stay away longer."

Rebecca had some questions when Cheryl got back into the car. First, she wanted to know who the lady was and why she was taking pictures. Second, she wanted to see if the lady had kids she could play with.

"Well, I don't know how old her kids are, but that's something to think about, isn't it?" Cheryl answered.

There was only one problem with their exchange. Now that she knew who Ari was, Cheryl realized that the woman had nothing to do with what had happened to Rudy. As impossible as it seemed, everywhere Cheryl looked appeared to be a dead end.

As the kids played, Cheryl got started with dinner, making a big pot of soup. She usually made a double batch and froze half of it. Naomi had taught her that trick, but now she had a better idea.

"Kids, we're going to take some dinner over to Miss Astrid next door. Can you grab your shoes and coats?"

As she peered out the window, Cheryl decided they should drive over. It wasn't that far of a walk, but she couldn't keep up with Matthew and carry the basket with the soup and bread. He never walked in a straight line, and she didn't want to think of what would happen if he veered off to the road or into a ditch.

Cheryl picked up her cell phone to put it into her pocket. It was then that she saw she'd missed a call a few hours earlier. She didn't recognize the number. An inner nudge told her to check the message because it might have something to do with Levi's case.

She navigated over to her voice mail and then lifted the phone to her ear. "Cheryl, this is Astrid." The voice sounded timid, weak. "First, I wanted to let you know that the doctor said Rudy is improving. But second, I also wanted to tell you that I looked through Rudy's email. I discovered that it was his relative's idea to sue Levi. This person told Rudy that if he couldn't get the money he deserved from the sale of our land, he'd get it another way. I'm going to talk to the police about this too. I just wanted you to know."

He. Astrid had said "he." But who? Was this family member someone Cheryl knew? Also, Astrid had said she would talk to the police about this. Had she already called them?

Cheryl considered calling Astrid back but then decided just to talk face-to-face, since she was already heading that direction. The image of the man with the wire-rimmed glasses filled her mind. Todd Arnold was in on this, she just knew it. He would have known that Rudy wasn't the one who filed the lawsuit. And there was another motive for him. As the lawyer, Mr. Arnold would get his cut too.

The kids thought it was an adventure to drive from one driveway to the next, but as they turned onto the country road, a sinking feeling settled in Cheryl's gut.

Todd Arnold was leaving the Wight place. She would know his fancy silver Cadillac anywhere. Something inside Cheryl told her to follow the man. Thankfully, she had insisted the kids get buckled into their car seats even though they were just going next door.

As she followed the Cadillac to town, Cheryl kept her distance. She called Naomi and asked her to come along, and when she passed her in-laws' farm, Naomi met her at the road and climbed into the car. She wondered if Todd had any idea that they were following him as he drove to a part of Sugarcreek she wasn't familiar with. It was a small neighborhood of older houses.

Todd pulled into a driveway. Cheryl tried to be as inconspicuous as possible. As he parked, she drove past him and stopped under a tree a few houses down.

Turning around in her seat, Cheryl tried to get a better look at the house. Then Rebecca's questions started in again.

"Mama, I thought we were going to see Miss Astrid. Why did we go to town? Matthew said he's hungry. Do we get to go home and eat our soup too?"

"Oop!" Matthew shouted louder and louder, pointing to his mouth.

Cheryl attempted to ignore her children and instead focus on the house where Todd Arnold had just parked. When she looked at the mailbox in front of the house, Cheryl's brow furrowed. The name on the mailbox was Wight. Chills ran up her arms, and she knew that somehow all the pieces were going to click together. She didn't precisely know how, but she knew that they would.

Cheryl was glad she had picked Naomi up along the way. Naomi knew everyone in town. "Naomi," she said, "I have a question. Do you know this street? I've never been to this part of town."

"Oh yes, I am familiar with it. Seth and I have driven down this road many times."

"You see that house back there? The name on the mailbox is Wight—W-I-G-H-T, just like Rudy. Do you know who lives there?"

"Oh yes. Gladys Wight. I do not know why I didn't put the pieces together before. Gladys is Rudy's mother, isn't she?"

Cheryl turned to Naomi with wide eyes. "Do you know anything about Gladys?"

"Well, I do know she had a nephew she took in. She raised him like a son after her younger sister died. I think I heard that he recently moved back in with her to help care for her. She had a fall a few months ago, I believe."

"That's curious that a nephew would come into town to take care of her, even though Rudy and Astrid are right here."

Naomi heaved a heavy sigh. "Ja, but you know how families are. Sometimes they are fractured in ways that outsiders can't understand."

Cheryl knew Naomi was talking about Sarah. "Yes, that makes sense, I suppose."

As they talked, the kids became more and more restless. By this point Matthew had decided he wasn't going to be happy unless he ate within the next thirty seconds, so Cheryl had Naomi unwrap the loaf of bread and break off chunks for him and Rebecca. That would buy her at least ten more minutes before they started up again.

From the corner of her eye, Cheryl saw movement, and as she watched, Todd Arnold helped an older woman into his car.

"Naomi, look." Cheryl pointed to the movement behind them, and then she twisted back to sit properly and did a U-turn. She drove to Gladys Wight's house and considered parking in front of the driveway so that Todd couldn't leave, but decided against it with Naomi and the kids in the car. She couldn't risk him doing anything to hurt them. Instead, she parked a bit past the driveway and got out.

She bent down before closing the door. "Naomi, please stay here with Rebecca and Matthew." Then she turned to the kids. "Mama has to go talk to someone. I'll be right back. Then we'll go home, I promise."

Cheryl quickly walked up the driveway, trying to avoid the icy patches of snow. Todd had just gotten the older woman into the car when Cheryl approached. He slammed the passenger door and then paused as he spotted her.

"Mrs. Miller," he said through clenched teeth. "What a surprise."

"Are you surprised?" She lifted her eyebrows. "I suppose you didn't think I'd figure it out."

"Figure what out?" Todd took two steps forward and adjusted his wire-rimmed glasses.

"Figure out that you were pressuring Rudy and Astrid to sell. Figure out that you filed the lawsuit against Levi. Figure out that you're the one who messed with the platform, causing Rudy to fall."

He scowled. "Really, that's quite a story. Too bad it's your word against mine." He glanced back at the house with a frantic expression on his face. "Now, if you'll excuse us, we have an appointment to get to."

With quickened steps, Todd moved to the driver's side. It was then that Cheryl noticed smoke curling out from under the front door of the house.

"What did you do?" she yelled. "Did you start a fire?"

"Move!" he shouted, his face red. "You don't want those children in the car to see their mother run over, do you?"

Cheryl knew he wasn't joking, and she ran back to the car. Her boot hit a spot of ice, and she nearly tumbled, but she caught her balance and continued on.

Cheryl jumped into the driver's seat. Only as she saw Naomi's face and heard Rebecca's cries joining Matthew's did Cheryl realize she was praying out loud, praying that God would protect them, and scaring the kids as she prayed.

Todd's car backed down the driveway, and he turned onto the road and sped past them.

Cheryl reached into her pocket, pulled out her cell phone, and thrust it at Naomi. "Call 911!"

She started the car and looked ahead, trying to see which way Todd Arnold was going. At the stop sign, he continued straight as if heading into town. As she followed him, Naomi gave Gladys's address to the dispatcher and told them the house was on fire.

Cheryl paused at the stop sign and then hit the gas. Just then, her car died and everything stilled. Hearing the silence, both kids stopped crying.

"Mommy, did we just run out of gas?" Rebecca called from the back.

Cheryl let out a moan and then followed it with a wry laugh. "See, Levi, this is why I need you out of jail now!" Over the years Cheryl had gotten used to him keeping fuel in her car. She'd been driving back and forth to town for over a week, and she hadn't looked at the gas gauge even once.

Glancing back over her shoulder, Cheryl could see that the house was now in flames.

She took the cell phone from Naomi and as quickly as she could went through her recent calls and found Chief Twitchell's number. She hit the call button and prayed that he would pick up.

When he did, the words came pouring out of her. "Chief, I think Todd Arnold is Gladys Wight's nephew, and he's living with her. I'm pretty sure he's been attempting to force Rudy and Astrid Wight to sell their house, and when they wouldn't he fabricated the lawsuit against Levi, and when that didn't get Rudy to budge, Todd removed the screws from the platform, causing serious injury to Rudy. But more than that, he has Gladys, and he's set her house on fire—"

The sound of a siren split the air, and a fire truck turned onto the street, stopping at the Wight house.

"Cheryl? Are you still there? Where are you? Who's with you?"

She turned her attention back to the chief. "Yes, I'm here. I'm at Gladys Wight's house, and the kids and Naomi are with me. We saw Todd Arnold drive off with Gladys toward town. You have to stop him, please!"

"We'll take care of Mr. Arnold, Cheryl. This is what you're going to do. I want you to stay in the car with your children and wait for an officer to come take your statement. We'll want one from your mother-in-law also. Don't go anywhere, don't talk to anyone, don't ask anyone any questions."

"I can do that," Cheryl said. She glanced behind at the children. Open-mouthed and speechless, they were fascinated by the activities of the firefighters. They weren't going to want to go anywhere anytime soon. Home and soup were forgotten.

"All right." Chief Twitchell paused for a few moments. "I've sent Detective Diaz your way. He should be there in about ten minutes."

"Okay, Chief," Cheryl said. She looked at Naomi, who was pointing to the gas gauge. "Um, maybe I could ask you a favor?"

"And what favor would that be?"

Cheryl squirmed in her seat. "I kind of ran out of gas."

There was a moment of silence, and then the chief chuckled. "Well, the Lord surely does work in mysterious ways, doesn't He? I'd say it was His way of keeping you out of trouble." She heard papers shuffling and then he said, "I'll have Diaz bring you enough gas to get to a station."

Cheryl thanked him, ended the call, and turned to Naomi. "The chief said we needed to wait here until Detective Diaz—Carlos—comes to take our statements." She shook her head. "It's not like we could go anywhere anyway. I'm sorry to involve you in this."

Naomi smiled. "I do not think you are the one who involved me in this, Cheryl. God knows my heart. I have been glad to help Levi by watching the children and doing household chores, but I have also longed to *do* something to help prove his innocence. I am glad to be here, in this place, right now, if it helps bring him home."

Cheryl smiled at her through tears. "It's really over, isn't it? Levi will be home for Christmas?"

Naomi reached across the console and took Cheryl's hand. "Yes. He will be home for Christmas."

Rebecca must have pulled herself away from all the excitement outside to hear their exchange. "Daddy's coming home?"

Cheryl laughed. "He is. And I bet he can't wait to have a piece of Christmas cake!"

Rebecca clapped her hands and cheered, and Matthew joined in. Naomi had just pulled out the bread again when a police cruiser pulled to a stop beside the car and Detective Carlos Diaz got out.

Cheryl opened the door and climbed out then shut the door behind her to preserve the heat in the car. "Hi, Carlos."

Carlos opened the trunk of the cruiser and lifted out a gas can. "Hello, Cheryl." He held up the can. "I can take care of this first, and then we'll have a talk."

Rebecca and Matthew excitedly peeked around—at the firefighters battling the blazing house, and at the very real and up-close policeman who was putting gas in their tank. Their little heads swung back and forth like they were watching a tennis match.

After Carlos put his gas can back into his trunk, he took Cheryl's statement. Naomi got Rebecca and Matthew out of the car and held their hands until it was time for her to give her statement, and Cheryl let the kids play in the snow right beside her. When the detective was through questioning them, they waited and watched the firefighters while he took a call from the chief.

When he walked back toward them, Cheryl asked anxiously, "How's Gladys? Is she safe?"

"Yes. We caught Mr. Arnold just outside of town. Take a breath, Cheryl. We have him. We're confident we have the right man."

"And Astrid? Is she safe too? Todd was just at her house."

"She wasn't home. She's safe, and the chief just spoke with her. She wanted us to know that because of you, she decided to talk to us about Mr. Arnold and her suspicions of him. She said she wanted to stop him from hurting anyone else. We're getting a search warrant for his home and office, and I'm sure we'll find further evidence to link him to the fire and to Rudy's fall."

Cheryl took a deep breath and looked up at the detective. "Does that mean my husband can come home?"

"Yes, Cheryl. It'll take a few days to get the truck out of impound, being a holiday and all that. But you can drive on over and pick him up. I'm sure those kids will approve."

And, judging by the way "those kids" rushed to the car when she told them they were going to go pick up Daddy, he was right.

CHAPTER TWENTY-FOUR

When Cheryl had started the Advent season, all she could think about was getting things done. She wanted to put up a tree, decorate, bake, and give her kids a Christmas to remember. As the days passed, however, none of those things mattered. The only thing she cared about was making sure Levi got home.

Yet, in the end, everything got done. The house was decorated, and a beautiful tree was up. Baked goods covered the countertops. A pile of presents had been tucked under the tree.

She had everything she needed and so much more. Because of how hard this Christmas had been, she realized, even more, how loved she was by the friends and family around her.

Cheryl felt as if she floated up the steps as she, Naomi, and the kids walked into the police station. Levi stood there. He had dark circles under his eyes. His face looked weary, and he needed a good shave. He looked a little thinner, and she guessed that he didn't get as much to eat here as he usually got at home. But none of that mattered. All that mattered was that he was free.

The kids swarmed him, and he dropped to his knees and gathered them in his arms. After a moment, he stood and hugged Naomi. The embrace lasted only a moment, as the Amish weren't fond of showing affection in public. But Cheryl had no such misgivings. She grabbed him around the neck in a fierce hug. Then, surprisingly, Levi lifted her head and kissed her on the lips, right there in front of everyone.

"Thank you, Wife." He chuckled. "Thank you for continuing to put your nose in other people's business."

Cheryl laughed through her tears. She knew that for as long as they lived, there would never be a more joyous Christmas, not ever.

The right person would also pay for his crimes. From what the chief said when they were gathering Levi's belongings, they had found some other crimes that Todd Arnold had run away from, and he likely wouldn't be getting out of prison for a very long time.

The news from the hospital was that Rudy was finally awake and was improving. Together, she and Levi would do what they could to help their neighbors. Sarah and Joe were also coming back into their lives. And they had their community, friends, and neighbors around them. Those who loved them, those who supported them, and those who showed them what a true Christmas blessing was all about.

Levi's blue eyes sparkled as she nestled closer for another hug. "Merry Christmas, Cheryl. God gave me a wonderful gift when He gave me you as my wife."

Two days later, Cheryl beamed with joy as she sat in front of the Christmas tree. Rebecca and Matthew ran back and forth from the kitchen to the living room.

"Is it time? Is it time?" they called. "Can we open our presents?"

"We will be opening our presents soon. But let's ask Mama which one she wants to open first," Levi said, walking into the living room.

While Judith and the Miller family, including Sarah and Joe, would be coming over later that day, Cheryl and Levi had decided to have an early Christmas morning celebration for just the four of them.

Cheryl knew which present she would choose to open first. She scooted some other gifts aside and picked out the ones from Aunt Mitzi. "Can I open mine?" She winked at Levi.

He laughed. "You are as bad as the kids. But yes, sure, go ahead."

Cheryl tore off the brown paper wrapping. She smiled when she saw an apron inside. It was a bright, colorful fabric that would always remind her of Papua New Guinea. Embroidered on the front was one word—*Serve*.

Cheryl released a happy sigh, thinking of Aunt Mitzi's words. "I can't think of anything more perfect. It's always the right time to do the right thing." *How did Aunt Mitzi know?*

When Rebecca and Matthew opened their presents a few minutes later, Cheryl was thrilled to see two small aprons similar to her own. The word embroidered on Rebecca's apron was *Grow*. And when Matthew unfolded his, it said, *Go*.

"Well, that is appropriate for our son," Levi said, scooting closer to his wife.

Cheryl tousled Matthew's hair. "I think Aunt Mitzi knows you well, buddy. You can wear this for the two minutes that you'll help Mama cook before you're off racing again."

Levi chuckled when he saw his present from Aunt Mitzi. It was a scarf that she had knitted. He wrapped it around his neck. "I could have used this while I was in jail. It was chilly there at times, but at least there were good parts of it too."

"Oh Levi, I'm not sure I'm ready for you to joke yet about your time in jail."

"Cheryl, it is not a joke. Just as God was working on your heart and having you serve and connect with our friends and neighbors, He allowed me to do the same in there. There are so many hurting men. I listened to a lot of stories. I have things that so many people want—family, home, faith. I was able to share about our lives, but mostly I shared about our God. I hate what happened to Rudy, and I hate what his cousin would try to do for financial gain, but I can see that God, indeed, had a plan to work everything out for good."

Cheryl and Levi sat side by side as they watched the kids open their gifts. She had genuinely never experienced such a wonderful Christmas as this one. She hadn't done half of what had been on her list—at least she hadn't done it herself—but through serving others and allowing them to serve her in return, she had realized what truly mattered.

An hour later, a knock sounded at the door, and Cheryl jumped to her feet. "Oh good, I think everyone is starting to arrive for Christmas lunch." Soon their house would be full, just as their hearts were full, and Cheryl wouldn't have it any other way.

AUTHOR LETTER

Dear Reader,

There is nothing more wonderful at Christmas than to spend time with family. As a mom of ten children—and many grand-children—I love the joy of decorating, baking cookies together, and seeing the delight on the little ones' faces when they open gifts.

Returning to Sugarcreek in the pages of this book seemed like coming home again. I loved spending time with Cheryl, Levi, and their growing family. Writing about Naomi, Seth, and others was also like catching up with old friends. I also enjoyed discovering new characters as I wrote. Judith has a special place in my heart for her loving and caring nature.

As I wrote this story, my heart was turned to those who may be having a difficult time at Christmas. We often have neighbors and friends who are struggling, and yet we really don't know unless we reach out. I've found that if someone comes to my mind, it's often a message from God to reach out to that person. A phone call or a visit, a plate of cookies or a note, can make a huge differ-ence in someone's life. The Amish proverb, "Good intentions die unless they are executed," is one we should all heed. Today is the day both you and I can make a positive difference in someone's life. Writing this story has reminded me to do so more and more. My hope is that you will be inspired to do the same.

Blessings,
Tricia Goyer

About the Author

Tricia Goyer is a speaker, podcast host, and *USA Today* best-selling author of over eighty books. She writes in numerous genres, including fiction, parenting, and marriage, as well as books for children and teens. She's a wife and a homeschooling mom of ten. She loves to mentor writers through Write that Book with Tricia Goyer: triciagoyer.com/write-that-book/. Tricia lives near Little Rock, Arkansas.

Fun fact about the Amish or Sugarcreek, Ohio

For many years members of the Amish and Mennonite communities have proven their "belonging" by keeping track of one another through a weekly newsletter called *The Budget*, which is published in Sugarcreek. News is written by local scribes and shared in a simple newspaper format. Interesting events, tragedies, humor, and everyday moments are captured and shared.

The Budget serves two distinct purposes: as a national Amish newspaper and as a local newspaper for the Sugarcreek/Holmes County area in Ohio. In addition to news from settlements around the nation, there is also news from Amish settlements on foreign soil like Belize, Israel, and Nicaragua.

Something Delicious from Our Sugarcreek Friends

Soft Caramel Cinnamon Rolls

This recipe is a favorite from my Amish friend Sherry Gore.

Ingredients:

1 3-ounce box cook & serve vanilla pudding	½ teaspoon salt
½ cup butter	1 tablespoon vegetable oil
2 packets yeast	6 cups bread flour
2 teaspoons sugar	butter
½ cup warm water	brown sugar
2 eggs, beaten	ground cinnamon

Directions:

Cook pudding according to package directions. Add butter and let set until lukewarm. Meanwhile, dissolve yeast and sugar in warm water until foamy. Combine pudding mixture with eggs, salt, oil, and yeast mixture. Mix well. Gradually add enough flour to make a soft and somewhat sticky dough. Knead well. Place back in bowl and cover with towel. Let rise forty-five minutes. Roll out onto clean countertop. Spread with generous amount of melted butter and cover with brown sugar and cinnamon. Roll up and cut into 1½-inch pieces. Place in greased baking pans. Bake for 15–20 minutes, until golden brown. Frost with caramel icing.

Caramel Icing

Ingredients:

½ cup butter

1 cup brown sugar

¼ cup milk

2 cups confectioners' sugar

Directions:

In a small saucepan, bring butter, milk, and sugar to a boil. Cook over medium heat for two minutes. Cool, then stir in confectioners' sugar.

Read on for a sneak peek of the first book in an exciting
new mystery series from Guideposts Books
—Secrets from Grandma's Attic!

History Lost and Found
by Beth Adams

"Tracy?" Tracy Doyle's husband, Jeff, appeared in the doorway, silhouetted against the sunlight that streamed in through the oversized front windows. "They're going to be here any minute." He tilted his head, as if trying to understand why she was sitting down.

"I know." Tracy sighed. It had been a long week, but there were still things that needed to be done before her sister, Amy, and her kids arrived for Matt's birthday party. First, she needed to put drinks in the tub of ice, then add the finishing touches to the Spider-Man cake. But Tracy had gotten distracted. She held Grandma Pearl's Bible in her hands, the pages worn soft with use. She'd recently found it in the attic, where well-meaning relatives had moved items from Grandma's bedroom after she'd passed. "I was just wondering about Jana and Matt."

"What about Jana and Matt?"

"I never really paid attention to the family records pages in Grandma's Bible before, but I was looking up a verse to read to

Matt tonight and saw it in there, and that got me to thinking." She indicated the "Births" page, which was carefully filled out in peacock-blue ink. "I was wondering when we should add them to the family tree."

Grandma Pearl had carefully recorded each member of the family, starting with her great-grandparents. She'd also written the date of her own marriage and the birth dates and marriages of each of her children and grandchildren. There was Tracy's name, with her birthday recorded in Grandma Pearl's sure hand, and the date she'd married Jeff, as well as the birthdays of their kids, Chad and Sara. Her cousin Robin's birth and marriage were there, as was the birth of her son, Kai. And there was Amy. She'd never married, but her two foster children had quickly became family.

"Maybe it's best to wait until the adoption is finalized," Jeff said.

Tracy knew that was the logical answer. Jana and Matt felt like family, but they weren't yet—not officially, anyway. Their adoption still had to work its way through the Missouri legal system before it would become final. But Amy loved them like they were born to her.

"You're probably right," Tracy said. She started to push herself up, but then she noticed something else on the page.

"What?" Jeff was watching her, his eyes narrowed.

She didn't answer right away. She looked down at the page, trying to understand. She was reading it correctly. But it made no sense.

"Grandma listed each of her children," Tracy said. "Ruth, Abigail, and Noah."

"Right…"

"But there's a fourth name here. Ezekiel Collins."

"Under your grandmother's name?" Jeff stepped forward.

"Yes. Under her and Grandpa. Just like he's another one of their children. But who in the world is Ezekiel Collins?"

Did Tracy have an uncle she'd never heard of? But how was that possible? Why would Grandma or Grandpa never have mentioned him? And yet there he was, recorded in Grandma's Bible in Grandma's handwriting. It couldn't be a mistake.

"That's strange," Jeff said, studying the page. But before he could say anything more, the doorbell rang. A second later the door opened, and Jana and Matt ran into the house and right through the parlor to the living room, where a stack of birthday presents waited. Tracy heard screeching as the children saw the gifts.

"They've decided they don't need to act like guests," Amy said, stepping in behind them. Jeff followed the kids into the living room and was already riling them up, urging them to guess what was inside each box.

"They're absolutely right," Tracy said. She closed the Bible and walked over to the front door and pulled her sister into a hug. "How are you?"

"I'm fine. The kids are a little bit excited."

"As they should be. It's not every day a boy turns ten."

Amy pulled back, and Tracy saw that her sister had dark circles under her eyes and her hair was past due for a trim. But she looked happy. Raising two active kids would do that to you.

"Matt told me on the way over that this is the first real birthday party he's ever had."

"That's really sad." The news hit Tracy like a punch to the gut.

"It's awful, isn't it?" Amy shook her head. "Their birth parents...Well, I imagine they did the best they could under the circumstances."

Amy was being charitable. Tracy didn't know the full story, but she understood that drugs had played a part in how Jana and Matt ended up in foster care.

"Thank you for doing this."

"Now I'm sorry I'm not doing more. This is just a family party. If I'd known that, I would have invited his whole class and rented a bouncy house and hired a clown and—"

"Clowns are creepy. This is perfect, Trace. Thank you." Amy looked down at the Bible that was still in Tracy's hands. "Doing some light reading?"

"Something like that." And then, after a pause, she said, "Hey, have you ever heard of someone by the name of Ezekiel Collins?"

Amy's brow wrinkled. "I don't think so. Who is he?"

"He's listed here in Grandma's Bible." Tracy opened to the records page and showed it to Amy.

"What in the world?" Amy looked up, her eyes wide. "Do we have an uncle we never knew about?"

"It kind of looks like that's what this means."

"How is that possible?" Amy asked.

"Can we open the presents now?" came a cry from the living room.

"Not yet," Amy called back. "You have to wait until your cousins get here."

"When will they get here?" Jana asked on Matt's behalf.

"Soon," Amy called. Then, to Tracy, she said, "When will they get here?"

"Soon." Tracy smiled. Chad and Sara were coming with their families, and Robin and her family would be here shortly as well. Tracy decided to put the question about Ezekiel out of her mind for now. She had an excited ten-year-old ready to enjoy his first birthday party ever. She needed to focus on him.

Tracy walked toward the bookshelves that lined the far wall of the parlor. Grandma Pearl had loved books, and the shelves were filled with hardcover editions of the classics as well as newer fiction, history, biographies, and a whole shelf of Christian titles. Tracy hoped to read through the entire collection someday. But that day would likely be far in the future, the way things were going. She bent down and set Grandma Pearl's Bible on the shelf. She'd focus on Matt now and worry about Ezekiel later.

⁂

Tracy had hoped to sleep in Saturday morning after the big party the night before, but the birds outside her window woke her with the sun. It was going to be a beautiful day—she could already tell as she climbed quietly out of bed. It was a beautiful June day. Jeff could sleep through anything and would probably stay in bed for another hour at least. She padded down the creaky staircase into the kitchen and started the coffee.

They had been renovating Grandma Pearl's Victorian home since they'd inherited it. Bit by bit, they were scraping off decades of wallpaper, retrofitting bathrooms, and realigning floors, uncovering all kinds of secret nooks and crannies hidden behind haphazardly constructed walls in the process. The kitchen was the room Tracy insisted they tackle first, and the big windows, gleaming white cabinets, and smooth granite-topped island still made her happy, every morning.

As the coffee brewed, Tracy fed their goldendoodle, Sadie, and spent some time reading her Bible and talking with the Lord. Then, fresh coffee in hand, she set about making her list of Saturday morning chores. There was laundry to do. And the bathrooms could use a good cleaning. She needed to vacuum after last night's party. Her library book was overdue. It had been a busy week at the newspaper, and with the party to prep for, she wasn't as on top of her to-do list as she would normally be. Then, there was the faculty lunch at the dean's house she and Jeff had to attend. And she'd promised Jeff she'd stop by the hardware store to get stain to refinish a dresser he'd found in the attic.

But even as she wrote, her mind kept drifting back to the name she'd found in the Bible last night.

Who was Ezekiel Collins?

Was Collins a middle name or a surname? If a surname, why would his be different than the rest of the Allen family? Had he died at birth and never been mentioned? What if he had run away or disgraced the family and been disowned? But Grandma would never do that. And Tracy's father would have surely mentioned him at some point. She couldn't figure it out. If she had another uncle, wouldn't she know about him?

Then Tracy had an idea. She glanced at the clock over the stove. The library would open shortly, and she needed to return her book anyway. She might not have the slightest clue who Ezekiel Collins was, but someone knew. There must be a record of him somewhere. And the Canton Public Library would be the best place to start.

Tracy made herself toast and eggs, and by the time she went back up the stairs to get dressed, Jeff was getting ready for his morning run. She'd never understand how that man could hop out of bed and go off and run three miles, but he did it almost every day.

"I'm headed to the library," she said, and he nodded, unsurprised. She did spend a lot of time there, she supposed. Jeff adjusted his earbuds and waved before he left. She dressed quickly and went downstairs, and then she walked out onto the porch and into the beautiful day.

The sun was warm on her skin, and the magnolias and primroses were in full bloom. Just before she climbed into her car, she looked back up at the house. It really was a gorgeous old Victorian, with its tall turret and generous front porch shaded by mature poplars and maples. Sometimes she still couldn't believe she got to live here.

She backed slowly out of the driveway. Tree limbs heavy with fresh green life arched over the street, shading the lovely old homes as she drove. Lewis Street was bustling, the sidewalks crowded with people enjoying the warm day. There was a line outside PJ's, as there was most days when his biscuits and gravy was on the menu. PJ kept saying he was going to remodel and add more tables, but Tracy knew that half the reason people came was for the battered wooden tables and booths that had been there for a hundred years. Robin's antique shop, Pearls of Wisdom, was open, and Jeannie's new bookshop looked to be doing a brisk business. Tracy was glad. Jeannie had worked so hard to rebuild after the fire, and now the shop was better than ever. She passed the newspaper office where she worked part-time during the week, and then the florist and coffee shop.

There were plenty of parking spots outside the library, which was housed in a historic brick building downtown. Tracy stepped inside, heading for the computer terminals. She returned her library book and waved at Grace Park, the head librarian, who was seated behind the checkout desk. As an investigative reporter, Tracy was very familiar with the research tools available at the library. She would start by searching their collection of newspaper archives.

"Hi, Tracy." Pastor Gary Bennett walked up to her, his two young grandchildren in tow. He always looked so formal when he was preaching, with his suits and ties, but right now, he just looked like a proud grandpa.

"Hello, Pastor." She glanced at the group of parents and toddlers gathering in the children's section. "Story time?"

"Indeed." He laughed. "And you look like you're on a mission."

"I am, I suppose," she said. Then she paused. Pastor Gary had been around Faith Chapel for decades. He'd been very close with Grandma Pearl. If anyone would know who Ezekiel was, Pastor Gary would. "I'm actually hoping to find out who Ezekiel Collins is—or was."

He recognized the name—that was clear. He startled, and his eyes widened.

"What makes you want to look into Ezekiel Collins?" he asked. His youngest grandchild, Henry, tugged on his hand.

"I found his name in Grandma Pearl's Bible." She watched as he shifted his weight from one foot to the other. "Do you know who he is?"

The words hung in the air just a bit too long before he answered.

"I don't," he finally said. "But I have to admit, Ezekiel Collins is a name that I've long wondered about."

Tracy wanted to ask a thousand questions, but she stayed quiet, waiting for him to go on.

"I have no idea who he is," Pastor Gary continued. "But he sends a sizable check to the church every month. I'd sure love to know who he is and why he sends that money."

A Note from the Editors

We hope you enjoyed another exciting volume in the Sugarcreek Amish Mysteries series, published by Guideposts. For over seventy-five years, Guideposts, a nonprofit organization, has been driven by a vision of a world filled with hope. We aspire to be the voice of a trusted friend, a friend who makes you feel more hopeful and connected.

By making a purchase from Guideposts, you join our community in touching millions of lives, inspiring them to believe that all things are possible through faith, hope, and prayer. Your continued support allows us to provide uplifting resources to those in need. Whether through our online communities, websites, apps, or publications, we strive to inspire our audiences, bring them together, and comfort, uplift, entertain, and guide them.

To learn more, please go to guideposts.org.

Find more inspiring fiction in these best-loved Guideposts series!